ANNIE'S ATTIC MYSTERIES®

Emeralds
in the Attic

Jan Fields

Annie's
Attic®

AnniesMysteries.com

Library of Congress-in-Publication Data
Emeralds in the Attic / by Jan Fields
p. cm.
ISBN: 978-1-59635-388-6
I. Title
                        2011905660

AnniesMysteries.com
800-282-6643
Annie's Attic Mysteries™
Series Creator: Stenhouse & Associates, Ridgefield, Connecticut
Series Editors: Ken and Janice Tate

10 11 12 13 14 | Printed in China | 10 9 8 7 6 5 4 3 2 1

— 1 —

Annie Dawson stood on the flagstone walk and stared at the porch of Grey Gables, the Victorian-style home she'd inherited from her much-loved grandmother Betsy Holden. As Betsy grew older, the big house became too much for her to keep up, and Annie had found it a bit tired and faded when she moved to Stony Point, Maine, to take care of her grandmother's estate. She'd worked hard for more than a year to bring Grey Gables back to the beauty the house had held during her childhood summer visits. She was proud of what she'd done to restore the house.

Until now.

Brightly colored mums in green plastic pots filled up most of the space around the porch's well-worn wicker chairs and table. More pots completely blocked the front door. "Well, they're certainly pretty," she muttered as she looked across sea of gold, burnt orange and deep burgundy flowers. On the upside, she decided, no one could possibly get to her door now to tempt her with the next school fund-raiser.

She turned as she heard the crunch of wheels on the gravel drive. Ian Butler's blue pickup rolled up the drive, showing that this must be an off-duty day for Stony Point's mayor. When the door opened, Ian's miniature schnauzer leaped out and raced for Annie, barking joyfully.

"Tartan!" Ian stepped out of the truck and shouted to the little dog. But Tartan excitedly ignored him, wagging his stubby tail with his whole body as Annie scratched his soft ears. Ian caught up and snagged the end of the leash. "I should have named him 'Greased Lightning.'"

As Tartan began snuffling through the leaves around Ian, Annie tried to dust off her favorite ratty yard-work jeans without drawing too much attention to their thread-bare knees.

"Thinking of going into the flower-selling business?" Ian asked, looking quizzically at the crowded front porch.

"No, I'm the victim of the high school fund-raiser. First, I bought three from Kate Steven's daughter, Vanessa. Then the other girls from the teen needlecraft group came by with their fund-raiser forms. I didn't want to look like I was playing favorites."

A slight smile crooked the corner of Ian's mouth. "I didn't know there were so many girls in that crafting group."

Annie sighed. "I suspect my name has somehow gotten on the 'soft touch' list at the high school. I bought one from everyone who came by. The flowers weren't very expensive, so I thought they'd be smaller."

Ian lost the struggle to keep a straight face and burst into laughter. Tartan looked up at his master and barked. "Annie Dawson," Ian said, trying to regain control. "You are a breath of fresh air around here."

"I'm not certain it's good politics to laugh at your con-stituents," Annie said, smiling. "I'll make you help me figure out what to do with all of these."

Ian pulled a cell phone from his pocket. "Now that I

might be able to do. How many would you really like to keep?"

Annie looked over the forest of flowers. "Maybe six?"

Ian put the phone to his ear while he made a quick count. "Hello, Ms. Booth?" he said. "This is Ian Butler. I was wondering if you might like some mums to help decorate for the ball?"

Annie squatted down and picked leaves out of Tartan's beard as Ian chatted with Liz Booth, president of the Stony Point Historical Society. She hoped he wasn't going to mention how silly she'd been to buy so many flowers. Liz always seemed like the kind of woman who'd never had a silly moment in her life. Annie smiled with relief when he only told her the flowers would be a donation from Annie Dawson.

"She's sending someone over with a truck to pick them up," he said as he looped Tartan's leash over a stout branch on one of the yew shrubs flanking the porch steps. The little dog immediately dove under the bush to sniff. "Let me help you move the ones you don't want to donate."

"Thank you," Annie said, handing him two pots of gold flowers. She grabbed two of the orange ones and headed over to the side yard where a small circle of cement covered her well access. "I really only wanted a few to hide this. I still haven't decided on what I want to get as a more permanent camouflage."

"At least it's fairly small," he said, "and not very noticeable."

Annie laughed. "Actually, I notice it every time I walk on this side of the house. It's probably one of those things a homeowner just assumes everyone is appalled by."

"So are you finally feeling really at home?" he asked.

Annie set her mums down and turned to take the ones Ian carried. She glanced back at the stately house. "Yes, I really am," she said. "I mean, I always felt at home here. Gram made Grey Gables such a warm, homey place every time I visited. But when I first came back after she passed—well, the house felt so empty. For a long time, I wasn't sure I could ever recapture that comfortable feeling I had here. But I'm starting to feel like it's mine now as much as it was Gram's."

"You've certainly put a lot of work into this place," Ian said. "It needed some TLC."

Annie frowned a little as she nodded. She still felt a pang of guilt every time she thought of how worn the house had grown in her grandmother's last few years. She knew she should have paid more attention, visited more, and not let things get that way. Even as the guilt seeped in, she heard Gram's voice in her head. "Don't waste time on the things that could have been," Gram always said. "Pay attention to the way things are and what you can do to make it better."

"I'm lucky I had Wally Carson," Annie said. "He's really helped make this place as beautiful as I could hope for."

"I'm glad to hear it," Ian said, turning back toward the porch. "What color for the last two? The burgundy?"

"Yes." Then before she said anything else, Ian had covered the distance back to the porch in a few long-legged strides and scooped up two beautiful burgundy mums.

"Are these good?" he asked, holding them up.

"Perfect."

As Ian brought them back, Annie took a moment to

admire how nice he looked in a softly faded, blue flannel shirt over a gray T-shirt and worn jeans. She shook her head with a smile, thinking of how grungy she felt in a very similar outfit while he just looked rugged. How did men manage to do that?

Ian set the flowers down and dusted off his hands. "That looks great," he said.

"So, I'm sure you didn't just come by to rescue me from buyer's remorse," she said. "Can I do something for you?"

"You can," he said. "And it's actually related to your mums in a way, since they're going to end up decorating the Harvest Ball. Have you heard about the ball?"

Annie nodded. "Mary Beth mentioned it the last time I was in A Stitch in Time. She said the Historical Society was having a charity ball at Maplehurst Inn. It's a little more than two weeks from now, right?"

"Right, on Saturday night," Ian said. "It's a masquerade. As mayor, I really have to make an appearance. It wouldn't be right if the mayor didn't come. I was hoping you would come with me." Before she could speak, he held up a hand. "Just friends, I promise. I'm just hoping my friend, Annie, will save me from an evening of looking woefully alone."

Annie laughed. "I doubt you could ever look woeful, Mr. Mayor. But a masquerade ball sounds like fun. I have no idea what I would wear though."

"It's a vintage ball," he said, "so everyone will be wearing something from the past. I imagine you have the best costume shop in the world for that." He pointed toward the attic window of the house. "Betsy Holden seems to have held on to everything else; surely you have something in the attic that would fit the theme."

"That's a great idea," Annie said. "I've seen some nice things as I've been trying to put the attic in order, and I know there are several trunks I haven't even gotten into yet. I may just find the perfect costume. What are you going to wear?"

"I have a tuxedo that belonged to my great-grandfather," Ian said. "It even has tails."

"How dapper!" she said with a grin, and then she gestured toward the house. "Would you like to come in for a cup of coffee?"

"Can we get in?"

"Well, we'll have to use the back door. Did Liz happen to mention when someone would be by for the flowers?"

"As soon as the poor guy is done making some sort of trellis for photographs at the ball, apparently."

Ian retrieved Tartan from foraging in the shrubs and followed Annie through the side yard and around to the back. Annie fetched a dish of water for Tartan, and they closed him in the mudroom. "Somehow, I don't think Boots would take kindly to a dog in her domain," Annie said. "And I'm not sure the house could take it if Tartan decided to chase Boots around for a while."

"I suspect Tartan wouldn't stand a chance," Ian said as they walked into the tidy kitchen. Light streamed through a window near the table and turned the warm, cream-colored walls almost white. Annie smiled at the effect. She loved autumn for the cooler temperatures without the gloom that would come with winter.

"Would you like an apple muffin with your coffee?"

she asked. "I made them this morning. I was feeling in the mood."

"Sounds like a good mood to me," Ian responded.

Just then Boots padded into the kitchen. She sniffed Ian's pant leg delicately, and then backed away. "Sorry," Ian said. "You probably smell Tartan." As Boots continued to glare at him reproachfully, the mayor laughed. "He's a nice dog, really."

The chubby cat sneezed as if dismissing the whole idea.

"I thought I was the only one who talked to cats," Annie said.

"I think Boots would bring it out in anyone. Though, I must admit, I talk to Tartan too."

Annie handed Ian the basket of muffins while she carried two tall mugs of coffee. They sat down and gazed out the window for a moment. The maples along one edge of the property seemed to have burst into flame practically overnight. The leaves glowed with orange, red, and gold.

She turned back to Ian. "So, what's been keeping the mayor busy?" she asked.

"Mostly this ball," he said. "The Historical Society is running it, of course, but they still seem to call me a couple times a day for one thing or another. This is a pretty big deal for Stony Point, I guess. Apparently the Historical Society is planning on some wealthy out-of-town patrons, so Liz Booth and her group are adamant that everything be exactly perfect. We're usually more of a potluck dinner sort of town. I'm not sure what to expect."

"I hadn't heard that much about it," Annie admitted. "I've been staying pretty close to home lately, getting the gardens ready for winter. I don't even know what charity the ball is going to support."

Ian nodded. "The money is going to the food pantry. The demand has been high for the last year. The economy hit some families pretty hard."

Annie nodded, feeling another nudge of relief at how her late husband had taken care that she was well provided for after he died. She still missed Wayne fiercely, but she appreciated that he'd always been the kind who looked ahead and planned. The changing economy didn't affect her too harshly, though she knew some of her friends in Stony Point were feeling the pinch.

"It's likely to get worse," Ian said. "If new regulations curtail the lobstermen any more than they already have, it's going to be hard for them to feed their families."

Annie looked up in surprise. "I hadn't heard about new regulations."

"That's because your brother doesn't have a lobster boat," he said with a rueful smile. "Apparently we have a pair of researchers visiting the area and running all kinds of tests. They go out with the boats and examine the catch. According to Todd, 'They get in the way of honest folks making a living.'"

"So new regulations aren't a sure thing?" Annie asked.

Ian shrugged. "Todd seems to think they are. But he's not exactly the family optimist." Ian glanced down at his watch and frowned. "I'm afraid I've got to grab Tartan and get going. I was only planning to take the morning off. I really need to get into the office and tackle some of the mayor's eternal paperwork."

Annie raised her eyebrows. "What time is it?"

"Nearly one."

"I have to get going!" Annie yelped. "I have a Hook and Needle Club meeting this afternoon."

Ian smiled. "I thought those were usually in the late morning. I know I've caught you for lunch or coffee at the end of more than one of them."

Annie raised an eyebrow. She hadn't realized Ian was paying such close attention to her schedule. "Mary Beth had a yarn shipment coming in this morning, but she didn't want to cancel the meeting entirely because she has some mysterious project for us."

"Ah—and I know how you like mysteries."

"I like them when they don't get me in trouble," she said.

"Good luck with that," Ian said, making Annie laugh. She had found more than a little trouble with the mysteries she'd stumbled into since moving to Stony Point.

2

Annie waved from the front yard as Ian drove away. "I'll certainly be glad when I get my front porch back," she murmured as she trotted through the side yard. By the time she reached the back door, she was mentally counting off the things she needed to do: shower, change, collect her needlework bag, grab another muffin. She nearly tripped as Boots darted between her legs in the kitchen.

"OK, OK," she said. "I'll add 'feed the cat.'" Boots rushed between her legs a second time, and Annie mentally pushed "feed the cat" higher on the list. She poured dry food into the small ceramic bowl and the chubby cat dove in. Annie reached down to rub the cat's head, but Boots backed away, sniffing Annie's hand suspiciously.

Annie laughed. "Tartan really is nice," she said. "But I'll go shower, Your Highness. I promise you won't have to smell dog any more."

A half hour later, Annie was dressed in a tailored pair of fawn-color corduroy slacks and a soft sage sweater set. It wasn't quite time to break out the thick fall sweaters she'd crocheted last year. She knew that time was coming though; the perfect balance of cool and color lasted only a short time.

She hoped to finish her present project before the weather turned much cooler. She loved the gorgeous forest green yarn she'd picked, but the twisted cable pattern itself had tested her crochet skills fiercely. *It's the Hook and Needle Club's fault*, she reminded herself as she grabbed her needlework bag. They were always encouraging her to push her limits, and they clearly believed in her skills more than she did.

As she once more circled the house to reach her car, Annie had the grateful thought that if she got stuck on the tricky stitches, she could count on Kate Stevens to help her out. Kate made the most gorgeous crocheted clothes that Annie had ever seen, and most of them were original designs. A Stitch in Time often featured Kate's unique pieces for sale. In fact, Annie had indulged in one of Kate's woolly jackets and looked forward to wearing it again this year when the temperature dipped a bit more.

She was still musing on clothes and needlework when she pulled into the last parking spot near A Stitch in Time. She hopped out of her car and walked across the sidewalk, peeking in the shop window when she reached it. As she expected, the other ladies were already seated in the circle of comfy chairs that the shop owner, Mary Beth Brock, kept set out for them.

She saw five of her friends had already pulled out their projects, and she smiled at the knitting needles flashing in Stella's and Gwendolyn's hands. Annie had never been much of a knitter, but she admired the way those two could turn out perfect rows as if by magic. She also noticed that everyone leaned slightly forward, and she suspected she was missing an interesting conversation.

The tiny bell over the door jingled as Annie rushed in. She heard Kate's quiet voice. "I'm not planning to go, but

Vanessa is desperate for me to buy her a ticket." Kate pushed a bit of her dark, straight hair behind her ear. "I would suggest she get the money from Harry, but he said they've had some small hauls on the boat lately and money's tight. Still, Vanessa wants to go so much."

"Wants to go where?" Annie asked as she settled into her chair.

"The Harvest Ball," Mary Beth said. "It has the whole town in a tizzy."

Gwen Palmer paused in her knitting and absently smoothed the hem of the perfect dove gray skirt she wore. Annie always admired the older woman's unwavering sense of style. "John and I are going," Gwen said. "I didn't even have to twist his arm. He felt it was something the bank president should appear at. Of course, to me, it sounds like a lovely chance to play dress-up."

"It does sound wonderful," Peggy said, her round face wistful as she dropped her quilting project in her lap. The pieced place mat in warm autumn colors contrasted sharply with the candy pink skirt of her waitress uniform. As usual, she had gotten a short break from work at The Cup & Saucer to come to the needlework meeting, though instead of squeezing it in during the morning lull as usual, she had come after the lunch rush. The club was one of the few indulgences the busy young mother allowed herself.

"Are you going?" Annie asked her.

Peggy shook her head and began to tick reasons off on her fingers. "No tickets. No babysitter. No dress. And definitely no tux for Wally. Unless my fairy godmother comes by with some mice and a pumpkin, I'm definitely not going to be there."

Annie smiled. "I didn't grow pumpkins, and I'm pretty sure I don't have mice any more, but I might be able to help with the dress and the tux."

All eyes turned to her.

"While I've been organizing the attic, I've seen several trunks of really lovely old clothes. And there are still more trunks I haven't even opened yet," she said. "I am absolutely certain I saw a tuxedo. You might have to work on it some to make it fit Wally, but you're fantastic with a needle and thread. I'm sure you could manage, and you're welcome to anything we can find. I'm certain we could find dresses for both of us."

Annie's best friend, Alice, looked at her and smiled. "So you're going too?"

"Ian asked me." Annie felt a blush warm her cheeks as all the other woman grinned at her. She spoke as firmly as she could. "As a friend. He has to go to these things, and he asked me to go with him as a friend."

"Right," Alice said, her blue eyes sparkling with mischief. "That Ian Butler is always such a friendly guy. Not that he's asked me to any parties lately. Has he asked you, Mary Beth?"

"Not that I can remember," Mary Beth said.

The women laughed, and Annie felt her cheeks grow even warmer. Then Mary Beth took pity on her and drew the attention away from Annie and Ian. "I can babysit Emily for you since I'm definitely not going," she said to Peggy. "You know I love that little girl to pieces."

"Really?" Peggy said and her eyes suddenly swam with tears. "You are the best friends I could have. I would love to go. Let me talk to Wally about it."

"I'll donate the tickets for both of you," Stella Brickson said, drawing all eyes to her. As the oldest member of the Hook and Needle Club, Stella had a tendency to put on queenly airs now and then. Annie had found her quite frightening when they first met, but she'd come to understand that Stella's heart was warmer than her tone. The older woman drew herself up regally and said, "As a member of the Historical Society, I felt I ought to buy several extra tickets since it is a fund-raiser. I can give you two." Then she turned her eyes to Kate. "I would be happy to give you one for Vanessa too."

"Looks like we have a room full of fairy godmothers," Kate said. "Vanessa will be delighted. Apparently Mackenzie is going, so Vanessa was desperate to go too."

"Since we're on the topic of the ball, I want to show you my surprise," Mary Beth said. She got up and walked to the front counter. Only the top of her cropped, gray hair showed as she rummaged around for a moment, and then she brought back a cardboard box. She pulled out a white costume mask. The corner of the mask was attached to a long, slender stick so the mask could be held in front of the wearer's face instead of being held on by elastic like a Halloween mask. "The owners of Maplehurst Inn have decided to have an extra event related to the ball. It's going to be a charity auction to raise money for Alzheimer's research, and it'll be held this Saturday afternoon. They're going to auction off decorated ball masks. That will give those coming to the ball a chance to wear a one-of-a-kind mask, and the timing is to make it easier to coordinate the mask and your costume. I thought the Hook and Needle Club could do a few masks and donate them to the auction, so I had them send over a box of blank mask forms."

"Oh," Peggy said, clapping her hands. "That sounds like fun. I actually have a little bit of pink satin left from the quilt I made for Emily last year. I could cover a mask with it."

"Wait, I have a great idea," Gwen interjected, holding up a perfectly manicured hand. "Let's not talk any more about what we'll do on the masks. We should each do one in secret, and then see which one brings the biggest bid at the auction. It'll be a little contest among us. That could be fun."

"And mysterious," Kate added.

"And we do like mysteries," Mary Beth agreed.

"You know, we wouldn't have to invent our own mystery here if you'd just dig us up a new one," Peggy said, grinning at Annie.

"Give her time, she's about to go—*dum, dum, dum*— back into the attic," Alice said in her best creepy voice. "Which reminds me, can I come too? I have a dress, and you know I have jewelry since I could hardly go to a party without showing off some of my Princessa line, but I'd love to help you play fairy godmother."

"Sure," Annie said, giving in to the excitement of the group. "We'll make a party of it. Anyone else?"

"As much as poking in the attic sounds like fun," Mary Beth said, "I'm not going to the ball, so I'll skip."

"And I have all I need," Kate added. "I've been working on this vintage dress pattern that's all lace, and I'm doing it in this fine sparkly yarn. It'll be perfect for Vanessa's gown, and I'm sure I can finish in time."

"Do you have time to do a mask too?" Mary Beth asked.

"Absolutely," Kate answered. "In fact, I already have my mysterious secret idea in mind."

"I don't believe I'll need anything to add to my dress," Stella Brickson said and every eye turned to her.

"You're going to the ball?" Gwen asked.

"You don't need to sound so surprised," Stella answered, looking slightly insulted. "I am a member of the Historical Society, and this is going to be the social event of the fall season." Then the tiniest twitch of a smile flitted across her face. "Plus, much of my wardrobe could be considered vintage."

"This is going to be so much fun," Peggy said, beaming at the woman she considered a mentor. "I'm glad you're going to be there too."

"So," Annie said, turning to Alice. "Who are you going to the ball with? Is Jim Parker going to be in town?" Annie knew Alice still kept in touch with the handsome photographer who had visited Stony Point when he was working on a book.

"I wish," Alice said. "That would make it easier. No, I actually haven't decided yet who I'll go with. I'm only certain that I'm going. I hate to miss a chance to wear a mask and play dress-up."

"This kind of event does bring out the little girl in me," Gwen said. "I remember how much I adored playing dress-up when I was a child. I would totter around in my mother's shoes until she caught me and scolded me for the terrible scuffing I always gave them."

As everyone began to share dress-up stories, Mary Beth passed out the rest of the mask forms. She was just putting the box back behind the counter again when the door opened with another light jingle of the bell.

A slightly built young woman in her mid-twenties practically jumped through the door. She wore her hair pulled back into a high ponytail and a wide smile covered her small face. With her bright eyes and very pointed chin, she reminded Annie of a pixie.

"Oh, what a charming shop!" the young woman exclaimed excitedly. "It's just beautiful."

"Thank you," Mary Beth answered. "May I help you?"

"Yes, I need to buy some embroidery floss. I am working on this kit, but they didn't include enough floss." The young woman giggled. "Well, probably they did, but I had a few knots and had to pick some parts out. Cross-stitch is so much more complicated than it looks."

Mary Beth blinked slightly at the rush of words. "It can take some practice," she said. "Do you have the piece so we can match the colors? Or maybe the chart?"

"I have both!" The young woman rooted around in the huge bag she wore over her shoulder and pulled out a plastic bag with a squeal. Her enthusiasm reminded Annie a little of Tartan.

Mary Beth quickly helped her pick the colors she needed. Then the young woman turned toward the Hook and Needle Club group. "I think it's so nice that you have a spot where people can sit and work on projects," she gushed. "I never seem to have time to sit. Well, sometimes in the evenings, but then the light can be bad. That's how I get the colors mixed up."

"We actually have a needlework group that meets here," Mary Beth said. "This is the Hook and Needle Club."

"Oh, that's adorable!" The woman rushed over and thrust her hand out at Annie. "Hi, I'm Jenna Paige. Actually, I'm Dr. Jenna Paige, but that always sounds so old."

Annie smiled and shook Jenna's hand. "I'm Annie Dawson."

"Oh, Annie is such a nice name," Jenna said. Then thrust her hand at Alice.

"I'm Alice MacFarlane," Alice said. "So, you're a doctor?"

"Not a medical doctor," Jenna said with a shudder. "I totally could not poke around inside people. I'm actually a biologist. My partner and I are here studying the lobsters."

"Oh," Peggy interrupted. "I've heard about you. I'm Peggy Carson. I met your husband, I think. I work at The Cup & Saucer."

"Oh, Simon isn't my husband." Jenna giggled. "We're working together on the project. He said you had wonderful food."

"I don't cook it," Peggy said, smiling. "I'm a waitress, but I thank you on behalf of my boss."

"I haven't been in yet, but I plan to," Jenna said. "I want to go everywhere. This is such a nice town, everyone has been so friendly. Well, mostly everyone." Then she brightened and said, "Have all of you lived here your whole lives?"

"Why would you want to know that?" Stella asked, narrowing her eyes slightly at the young woman.

Annie remembered how much Stella didn't like anyone she considered "nosy."

Jenna just turned and smiled at Stella. "This just seems like the kind of town where families would settle forever." Then she thrust her hand out at Stella. "I'm so pleased to meet you."

Stella looked at her in alarm and didn't touch the hand. "Thank you. I am Stella Brickson," she said primly.

Kate stepped forward and took Jenna's hand. "Kate Stevens," she said. "I'm certain you're doing very important work out on the boats. We do want to keep our lobster population healthy."

"Yes," Jenna said, her eyes wide. "A healthy and vital marine environment is essential to life on earth."

Annie caught a sideways look and slight eye roll from Alice. Jenna Paige did seem amazingly high-strung, but it was hard to resist such a friendly girl, though it was clear Stella had no trouble resisting her. She continued to frown disapprovingly as Jenna chattered about the town.

"I just love your little town square," Jenna said. "And the lighthouse. I love lighthouses. Anyway, I still don't know—have you all lived here forever?"

"None of us are quite that old," Gwen said in an amused tone.

"I didn't mean that! Besides, I like old people!"

At that Alice burst out laughing. "I probably should go before my joints seize up," she managed to say. "Annie, when are we getting together for the costume search?"

"Costumes?" Jenna said.

"For the Harvest Ball," Peggy explained. "It's a charity ball."

"Oh, that sounds wonderful!" Jenna exclaimed. "Where is it? Are there still tickets?"

All eyes turned to Stella since it was the Historical Society putting on the ball, as Stella had been quick to remind them earlier. Stella finally sighed and began to explain the coming fund-raisers. From Jenna's bright eyes, Annie suspected she'd be seeing the young woman at the ball.

"Peggy, timing is really up to you," Annie said quietly, hoping not to draw the biologist's attention back to them. "When do you want to get together to look in the attic?"

"Could it be tomorrow afternoon?" Peggy asked. "Afternoons are slow right now at the diner in the middle of the week like this. I'll get the stink eye from the boss, but I'm sure I can get a couple hours off. Would that be all right?"

"It works for me," Alice said.

"Me too," Annie agreed. They quickly decided on the exact time, and then all three escaped while Jenna Paige's attention was centered raptly on Stella. Glancing back though the large window, Annie had to smile at the pained expression on the older woman's face.

— 3 —

When Annie pulled up at Grey Gables, she was delighted to find her porch empty of mums, though she could see it now needed a good sweeping. The yard was beginning to need raking too, but Annie wanted to wait a few days. She actually liked the look of the brightly colored leaves on the grass and the sound of the crunch under her feet. As long as she cleared them off before the next rain, she didn't feel in any hurry.

She stood on the front path, looking at the leaves drifting down and thought of the times she'd shared the raking with Wayne back in Texas. When their daughter, LeeAnn, was little, she'd begged them to make a big pile of leaves and let her jump in it. Even though it meant raking the same leaves over and over, somehow it never seemed like such an overwhelming task.

Missing Wayne fiercely still snuck up on her now and then, but she found the bittersweet memories were finally growing less painful. Her wonderful new friends in Stony Point had helped, but so had the ways she'd changed since coming back. She was reconnecting to her own past; her memories of summers in this very house with Gram and Grandpa were filling some of the empty places in her heart.

With a slightly teary smile, Annie hurried up the steps and into the house. She passed Boots curled up in a sunny spot in the kitchen. The cat twitched an ear but didn't bother to look up. *I guess I finally found a point in the day that Boots doesn't consider mealtime*, Annie thought as she walked to the mudroom and grabbed the broom.

After she swept the front porch and walk, Annie moved from one small chore to another, and the rest of the day passed quickly. She'd learned most of the important fall tasks last year, and now it was just a matter of doing each of them at the right time.

Sunset came earlier every day, and Annie always tried to be outside for it. The changing slant of the sun made for some lovely, though brief, sunsets. Living on the East Coast made the sun seem to leap up over the water in the morning and dive for cover every evening. Somehow that made each sunrise and sunset even more special and rare just because they were hard to catch.

The next morning, Annie was up before sunrise, and she stood on her porch sipping coffee as light painted the horizon over the strip of water she could see from the porch. Boots had slipped outside with her, zipping through the door like a shadow. Annie knew from experience that it didn't pay to chase the cat around to get her safely back in the house. It was easier to let her sniff around the porch. Since Boots hadn't had her morning bowl of dry food, she wouldn't linger outside if she thought Annie might be on the way to the kitchen.

"Morning, neighbor," a cheery voice called out.

Annie turned toward the sound to see Alice crossing the lawn that separated Grey Gables from what had been the carriage house when the whole place was much grander. Alice carried a small basket covered in a tea towel. "I see you come bearing treats," Annie said.

"You know I hate to arrive empty-handed," her friend replied. Annie smiled as she noted that Alice was wearing her "adventure clothes," which were nearly as worn as Annie's own yard-work gear.

"Our attic adventure doesn't start until this afternoon," Annie said. "You weren't planning on getting a jump start on Peggy were you?"

Alice shook her head. "I'm going to spend the morning cleaning," Alice said. "I've gotten a little behind with all the parties I've had booked lately."

Annie opened the front door and led the way into the house. As she expected, Boots followed them inside. "I'm glad to see the economy hasn't hurt your business."

"It was a little slow over the summer this year, even with the 'summer people' in town," Alice admitted. "I had to dip into my savings once or twice, but everything picks up in the fall. People buy for the holidays."

After Annie dug out the box of dry food for Boots, whose meows of starvation would have been difficult to talk over, she poured a mug of coffee for Alice and freshened her own cup. Alice unwrapped a lovely golden applesauce cake, and they sat down to chat.

Annie took a bite of the warm cake and moaned. "Have you thought of marketing some of your baked goods?" she asked. "I baked apple muffins yesterday, and they really can't begin to compete with this."

"I have thought about picking up some extra money baking, but then I think it would take away some of the fun. Right now, it's what I do to relax. And I'm not sure it would be good for my waistline to spend all day surrounded by sweet baked goods! I don't have that much self-control."

Annie smiled. "I can totally understand that. Your baked goods are dangerous."

"Are you going back to Texas for Thanksgiving?" Alice asked.

"Right now I'm trying to get LeeAnn and Herb to bring the twins here. I would love for them to have a Thanksgiving in Gram's house. My parents were in the United States on sabbaticals from the mission field for a couple of Thanksgivings when I was a kid, and we always came here whenever they were. Do you remember that?"

"Of course," Alice said. "I was horribly jealous because you got to eat your Gram's food. My mom was not a gifted cook."

Annie laughed. "Mine either. I think her mind was always somewhere else." Annie leaned back in her chair and peered at Alice over her coffee cup. "So, have you decided on a date for the Harvest Ball yet?"

"Since yesterday afternoon? No."

"Who are your choices?"

Alice squinted at her. "You can't laugh."

Annie drew a cross over her heart. "I promise."

"Well, Fred Macgruder has been hinting."

"The grocery guy's dad? But isn't he …"

"Old, scrawny and on oxygen," Alice finished. "Yes. He's sweet though and really funny. And I wouldn't be marrying him; it's just a party. But he's not my first choice because he probably can't dance."

"What with the oxygen tank and all," Annie said with a perfectly straight face.

"No laughing! My other choice is Stan Ward. He's a lobsterman, and he's also really nice. And has most of his hair. And can breathe on his own."

"So an A-list choice," Annie said.

"Sort of—" Annie raised her eyebrows. Alice sighed and continued. "He smells like fish. I think it's one of those things you can't get out of your pores or something. I'm not sure. We went to the movies a few weeks ago and … sometimes it's a little like dating Flipper."

"I see the problem," Annie said. "So just those two?"

Alice sighed again. "Last night Peter Warren called and asked me. He's associated with the Historical Society, and he's very nice looking. But I'm not sure he *gets* my sense of humor. Sometimes he gives me the exact same look my college biology professor gave me when I drew hats on all my frog lab drawings."

"Tough choices," Annie said.

"I wish Jim were in town," Alice said. "Then it would be an easy choice."

"If you could get Jim into a tuxedo," Annie said. "He looks like he might rebel."

"I have my ways of dealing with rebellion," Alice said.

Alice stayed a bit longer, and their conversation drifted to the work they had to do to get ready for the coming winter. Finally, they couldn't really put off the day any longer, and Alice hurried off. Annie spent the morning doing some light housecleaning, and then curled up with a novel and a warm lap full of cat until it was time for the costume hunt.

Eventually, Annie heard a car pull up in the drive. She shifted a disgruntled Boots over onto the couch and walked to the porch. Peggy hopped out of the car and waved. Alice must have heard the car in the drive because she was already crossing the lawn.

"I'm so excited about this," Peggy said. "Wally grumbled a little about the whole idea of dressing up, but he agreed!"

"That's great," Annie said, giving the younger woman a hug as she reached the top of the porch stairs.

"Wait until you see this attic," Alice said to Peggy as they walked into the house. "I believe Betsy Holden's attic is a little like the Smithsonian Institute."

Peggy looked at her quizzically and Alice laughed. "The Smithsonian is America's attic and this house holds Stony Point's attic. It looks like everyone in Stony Point gave Betsy something for safekeeping at one point or another."

"Betsy was like that," Peggy said. "You just knew you could trust her with anything." Then she grinned at Annie. "But it has also meant we've had a lot of mysteries around here since you came back to Stony Point."

"Well, today I'm closing my eyes to all mysteries," Annie said. "Except the mystery of what we will wear to the ball."

She led the women upstairs to the attic. Though the attic was no longer the mass of confusion it had been when Annie first walked into it after coming back to Stony Point, she still had boxes and trunks she'd never opened.

"It looks like you've sorted the boxes from the furniture," Alice said.

"Some," Annie agreed. "I donated a bunch of chairs to the thrift store since they were willing to come by and pick them up. Gram had stray chairs from at least three kitchen sets in here. Just moving those along helped some with making it look more organized."

"What's the dress on the mannequin?" Alice said, pointing toward the corner where a dressmaker's dummy was wrapped in an old sheet.

A hat perched on top of the dummy's "neck" giving the figure a spooky look. Boots had scared Annie half to death once swatting at ribbons trailing from the hat and making it move in a ghostly way.

"I've never unwrapped it," Annie said. "I don't think it's wearing anything we want—just look at that awful hat! But I do have my eye on some trunks that might just produce exactly what we're looking for."

"OK!" Alice said cheerfully. But she pointed at the mannequin, adding, "You really ought to do an unveiling of that some time."

Annie smiled. "I'm sure I'll look at everything in here someday."

They slipped through the tight rows Annie had made through the carefully stacked boxes until they reached a steamer trunk covered with peeling labels from around the world.

"Oh!" Peggy gasped. "What a wonderful trunk!"

"Isn't it?" Annie said. "I don't know why I haven't poked around in it yet. There are just so many things up here." She lifted a small leather suitcase from the top of the trunk, laid it off to one side, and then she flipped the trunk's heavy brass latches.

The women gasped as the first glimpse of bright scarlet

flashed as soon as light hit the trunk, and the women stared at it a moment in admiration.

The red satin dress looked like a style from the 1940s. The top of the dress was formed by two pleated strips that crossed in front leaving a low V-neckline, and then separated to go over the shoulders like extra-wide straps. Under these, a wide, smooth band circled the body just under the bust. Below that, two more wide, pleated bands crisscrossed the stomach. The skirt then fell smoothly to the floor.

"You should try that one, Peggy," Annie said. "With your dark hair and curves, it would be stunning on you."

"Do you think so?" Peggy answered quietly. "It's so beautiful."

"You'll make Wally's eyes fall out," Alice said with a laugh.

Peggy gently carried the dress to a cleared area of the attic where Annie kept the floor well swept and dust free. Earlier, Annie had set up a faded three-panel screen she'd found to make a temporary "changing room." Peggy stepped behind the screen and slipped into the dress. It looked as lovely on her as they had expected. She certainly filled out the bustline far more than either Annie or Alice would have.

"Do I look all right?" Peggy asked. "I don't want to look silly or … fat."

"The way the bands cross at the stomach is perfect for a curvy figure," Alice said, "and I'm sure Wally won't be looking that low anyway."

Peggy looked down, noticing the deep neckline. "Oh my. Maybe I'll pin that up some."

"So we've scored one quick success in the costume

search," Alice said, rubbing her hands together. "Now, back to the hunt!"

Peggy quickly changed back into her uniform and draped the gown carefully over the stair rail. "Annie, did you say you've seen a tuxedo up here?"

"Yes, now I just need to remember where." She stared across the mass of boxes and trunks, and tried to picture exactly which one held the tux. "I think it was in that trunk." She pointed to a spot deeper in the attic, and they wove their way to it.

Annie knelt and pulled open the lid. Just as she remembered, the handsome black tuxedo lay on top. Peggy gasped as Annie lifted it out. Unlike the tux Ian had described, this one did not have tails, though it did have lovely black satin lapels. Under the suit lay a slightly yellowed tuxedo shirt and a black satin cummerbund.

"Oh, Annie," Peggy said softly. "It's just perfect. Wally is going to look like James Bond!"

Annie and Alice exchanged a glance. As fond as they were of Wally, the shaggy-haired handyman didn't quite bring James Bond to mind. *Though*, Annie thought, *you never know what the power of a tuxedo might do.*

"Now we just need a dress for you," Alice said to Annie. "And some bling for you both—unless you want me to provide that. I probably have some Princessa jewelry you two could wear. You don't even have to pass out business cards, unless someone asks where you got it, of course."

Annie laughed. "You know I love your jewelry," she said, "but there's a box with costume jewelry in that trunk right there." She pointed a little farther up the attic. "I think I'll try vintage before I go for anything more modern."

"Just letting you know it's available," Alice said.

Peggy gave Alice a quick hug. "And we appreciate it." Then she looked down at the trunk. "What else is in this one?"

"I'm not sure," Annie said. "Once I saw it was clothes, I didn't really pick through it." She turned her attention back to the trunk and gently lifted several more nicely made men's dress shirts. "It looks like it's all men's clothes. Certainly that's all that's in this upper tray." She lifted the tray out of the trunk and set it off to one side. She heard Alice and Peggy gasp and quickly turned her attention back to the trunk.

On the top of the lower section of the trunk, a dress had been carefully folded. Annie reached out and touched it, feeling the slight cling of real silk. She lifted the dress, standing as it unfolded to a floor-length gown.

The dress was a pale green with a faint floral pattern in dark green, peach, peachy-rose, and lilac. It was cut on the bias and intended to fit close to the body all the way through the hips. The bodice was low and cut straight across; then a translucent short cape in the same pale print wrapped around, forming fluttery, short sleeves. The cape piece pleated and the ends met just above the waist of the gown. Pale silk cabbage roses formed from ribbon were pinned over the spot where the shawl met the dress.

The overall look was delicate and almost otherworldly. Annie fell in love with it immediately. "It's beautiful," she said softly.

"And you're definitely the only one I know with the tiny

figure to pull it off," Alice said. "You've got to try it on. I want to see."

Annie carried the dress carefully over to her temporary dressing area. She was almost afraid to breathe on the delicate fabric. She wondered if it might be too delicate to have survived storage for so long.

When she slipped into the dress, she was delighted to see it fit perfectly, and it seemed a bit less fragile than she'd thought from looking at it. None of the seams were frayed or strained. She stepped nervously out from behind the screen.

Peggy and Alice grinned, and Annie knew she'd found the perfect dress.

4

"All we need now is bling," Alice said cheerfully as Annie slipped back out of the silk gown.

"Let me just close up this trunk first," Annie said. She bent over the clothing trunk and spotted a flash of white satin peeking out from under another dress. She turned the dress back and found a pair of long white gloves. "Oh, Peggy, these would go wonderfully with your gown."

Peggy practically squealed when she saw them and quickly put them on. They were a little snug on Peggy's hands, but none of the seams looked stressed. "I think they're perfect," Peggy said. "You know, now I think I'd like to find a pearl choker. Don't you think that would make the whole thing perfect?"

Annie closed the clothing trunk and exclaimed, "On to the jewels!" She moved to a smaller trunk that lay stacked on a flat, steamer-style black trunk. When she opened the smaller trunk, the light from the window flashed on the array of costume jewelry in the upper tray.

"Oh, now that's bling," Alice said. She stepped close and lifted out an elaborate necklace that looked like a whole bouquet of flowers made from Bakelite with rhinestone centers. "I'm having trouble picturing the outfit that would be perfect for this."

"Oh look, pearls," Peggy said.

She pulled out two different strings and tried them on. "Do you think either of these would go with my dress?"

"I think both of them would," Alice answered. "Why don't you wear them together? Are there earrings to match?"

They poked through the piles of pins, necklaces, earrings, and bracelets until they found two matching teardrop pearl earrings. Like a lot of older costume jewelry earrings, they weren't made for pierced ears. Instead, the backing was tightened against the ear with a little screw. Peggy laughed as she looked at them. "They look like tiny versions of Wally's wood clamps. But they should be perfect with the dress."

"You could wear your hair up to show them off," Annie suggested.

Peggy nodded. "You know Lisa at the diner? She's going to cosmetology school in the evenings. She already volunteered to do my hair when I told her I was going to the ball. I have so many fairy godmothers!"

Annie smiled and turned back to the pile of jewelry. She thought a small string of pearls might be a nice companion for her dress as well, and she was pretty sure she remembered Gram having a necklace like that. As she looked over the mixed-up pile, she sighed. Nothing seemed quite right.

"Maybe there are more under the tray," Alice suggested.

Annie lifted the tray up and set it off onto the lid of the steamer trunk. She saw a couple of smaller jewelry boxes. One seemed to have only broken bits of jewelry and unmatched earrings.

"Wow, your grandmother really saved everything," Peggy said.

"I'm starting to think so," Annie agreed. "Though some of these might work as embellishments on our masks. You're welcome to use anything you see that appeals to you."

"Oh, good idea," Alice said, taking the box from Annie to poke through it with Peggy. They each grabbed a few pieces, laughing as they quickly hid them in their pockets.

Annie pulled another box from the small trunk. This jewelry box was flat and nearly square. The wood of the box was still beautiful, almost glowing in the sunlight coming through the window. Annie opened the box and found a lovely matched set of costume jewelry. A necklace, brooch, earrings, and a hair comb were nestled on a specially made velvet liner.

"Fancy," Alice said, peeking over her shoulder. "Look at all the emeralds. Those would look gorgeous with your eyes, Annie."

Peggy stepped closer to see. "They are pretty. I like the hair comb. But one of those earrings is definitely broken."

Annie picked up the broken earring and saw the screw backing for the earring had been wrenched off. "That's too bad," she said. "It's a lovely set."

"You could have them converted to pierced," Alice said. "I still say they would bring out your eyes. You should wear them to the ball."

The necklace looked like it would fall above the neckline of Annie's gown, but she suspected it was a little too elaborate for the dress. At second glance, she saw the pendant looked like a highly stylized golden tree with tiny emerald leaves and seed pearls that reminded her of spring blooms or fruit. The earrings repeated the pattern, but the "trunk" of each was a larger drop-shaped emerald that dangled from the small canopy of seed pearls and emeralds. In the brooch, the tree design was more elaborate, using more stones. And the hair comb mimicked the "canopy" of the tree but had thin golden loops added with pearls at the apex of each loop.

"I don't think so," Annie said. "I think Gram had a nice string of small pearls in her jewelry box in her room. And for earrings, I have a nice small pair of diamond earrings Wayne gave me. That's more my style. But I'll take these downstairs. I might use them for ..." she dropped her voice, "... my secret mask. So, are we all set?"

Peggy suddenly looked wide-eyed at Alice and Annie. "I forgot shoes! I don't have any shoes that would go with a dress like that!"

Alice looked down at the younger woman's feet. "I think I have a pair you can borrow," she said. "I love shoes! Come on over to my house, and I'll show them to you."

"Thanks." Peggy beamed again. "And thank you, Annie. I am so excited about this ball. But I need to grab the shoes and run. If I don't get going soon, I'm definitely going to be in trouble at work."

Alice helped Peggy carry the clothes down the stairs as Annie put the tray back in the small trunk and closed it up. She knew that if she left any of the trunks open, Boots would manage to sneak upstairs and run off with sparkling jewelry.

Annie picked up the small wooden jewelry box and her lovely gown and hurried after her friends. She laid the gown out on her bed, and then she closed the door so Boots wouldn't decide that she needed to nap in the middle of the dress.

They chatted another minute or two before Peggy and Alice set off across the lawn to the carriage house. As Annie looked after her friends, a chilly breeze blew in through the door, and Annie shivered. She closed the thick oak door, happy to be in the cozy house.

Then with a smile, she walked across to the living room and picked up the lidded basket where she had put things to use for the mask. The broken earrings had given her a perfect idea. She carried the basket into the kitchen to work at the sunny table and sip tea.

As the kettle warmed on the stove, Boots slipped into the kitchen and peeked into her bowl. "Sorry, but it's not mealtime," Annie said. The cat sat and wrapped her fluffy tail around herself before offering a questioning meow.

"You heard me. I need to stop feeding you every time you ask," Annie said. "It's not good for you."

Boots meowed again, and then walked over to flop in a sunbeam that lay across the floor. She rolled around in the sun, exposing a wide expanse of pale belly.

"That proves my case," Annie said, laughing. "Just look at all that belly!"

Boots rolled over again to show her back to Annie just as the kettle whistled. Annie poured the hot water over her tea bag and carried the mug to the table. She took the small mask out of her basket. She'd already covered the plastic form with a swatch of black satin she'd found in Gram's scrap basket, and she'd sewn little pearl beads all along the outer edge of the mask.

When she'd seen the broken emerald earring, she knew

it would be the perfect corner piece to help cover where the stick attached to the mask. She held the earring up to the mask and nodded. It would be great.

Carefully, she took the broken clip off the piece. As she looked it over, she realized it would look even better if she put some gold wire loops and pearls to add height at the corners like the loops on the emerald hair comb. And she wanted some black, white and emerald green satin ribbon to wrap around the stick and also to hang from the corner of the mask for even more movement on the finished piece.

"Well," she said. "Looks like I need to make a quick run to A Stich in Time. That's top on my list for the morning. But for now, I think I need some kitty time."

Boots looked up at her. "Mrrr-ow?"

Annie leaned over and stroked Boots's head, and then gathered all her bits back into the basket. She tucked the basket up on top of the fridge. Boots had been practicing her skills at getting into Annie's project bags and baskets lately. Annie was still missing a ball of the soft, forest green sweater yarn and hoped it would turn up soon as she wasn't sure if Mary Beth had any more in that dye lot.

She scooped up Boots and headed for the living room and a quiet evening of vegging out in front of the television.

On Thursday morning, Annie fully intended to get an early start into town, but Boots decided to help her straighten up her bedroom while Annie was in the shower. Of course, the cat's idea of a clean dresser was knocking everything on the floor. It had taken all morning to chase down everything, especially since she'd had to pull the dresser away from the wall to find some of it.

"That's the last time I leave you alone in a room," Annie scolded as she lugged the cat downstairs and plunked her on the couch. Boots gave a small, disgruntled meow before settling down for a nap.

Scooping up her keys, Annie headed out the door before something else popped up and needed her attention. She paused and patted the roof of the Chevy Malibu for luck before hopping in. She'd started that as a joke six years ago when Wayne had given her the car for Christmas.

"That little Malibu will last for years if you take good care of it," Wayne had said as he handed her the keys.

Annie had patted the roof of the car. "I will."

"I mean take care of it like a *car*," he'd told her as a slight smile had crooked the corner of his mouth. "It's not a pet."

"You never know," Annie had said. "Maybe cars appreciate a little petting too. I don't believe in taking chances."

Wayne had burst out laughing at that, but Annie made it a habit to pat the car whenever her husband was watching. She sighed now as she turned the key. She missed Wayne so much, but she liked to think he was still watching and laughing at her and her pet car.

The drive to A Stitch in Time was short, but Annie enjoyed the sight of the changing trees, almost glowing in the late afternoon sun, as she passed them. The maples were her favorites with their fiery colors, but even the poison ivy along some of the overgrown wooded lots was turning a beautiful bright red.

Traffic had lightened up considerably since most of the summer people had closed up for the season and headed south for the winter. She knew they'd have a burst of visitors when the leaf color really peaked, but the population of Stony Point was slimming down. More and more, the faces she saw on the street were ones she knew, or at least recognized from passing them before.

Annie easily found a spot almost exactly between A Stitch in Time and The Cup & Saucer. As she passed the front window, Annie noticed Mary Beth was the only person in the shop. That alone proved it must be fall. Annie never caught Mary Beth alone in the summer. Her friend looked up as the bell jingled merrily over the door.

"Ah, still haven't found the errant ball of yarn?" Mary Beth asked. Annie had told her about the kitty yarn heist nearly a week ago when it happened. "I finally had a chance to look through the cubby and I think I have one more skein in that dye lot."

"That's great. No, I haven't found the yarn, but I haven't given up. Still, I better buy the one you found. No telling just what damage Boots has done to the one she swiped." Annie pulled her list out of her pocket. "I actually came in for some secret supplies."

Mary Beth laughed as she leaned on the counter. "You aren't the only one. Gwen came in this morning, but I'm sworn to secrecy about what she bought."

"I finally have a real plan for mine so I need a few things," Annie said. "Didn't I see some nice gold wire here?"

"We have gold wire in several gauges. How well does it need to hold its shape?"

Annie explained her plan, and Mary Beth helped her pick the perfect wire. She also collected the ribbon she needed. Annie was delighted to see that Mary Beth had narrow satin ribbon in a perfect emerald green. They chatted while Mary Beth rang everything up and bagged it all in a plain brown paper bag, skipping over one of her clear bags with A Stitch In Time printed on the side.

"The old brown paper bags will help keep your secret," Mary Beth said. "In case you run into any of the other Hook and Needle folks." Then she looked toward the door and grinned. "Speaking of which."

Annie turned as Alice walked through the door. "Long time, no see, neighbor," she said.

"I ran out of sequins," Alice said, picking a few packages from Mary Beth's small stand display of common embellishment items.

"Oh, sequins," Annie said. "I didn't think about sequins. But, I'm happy with what I have. I will not be tempted."

"You know me, I'd be a great magpie," Alice said. "I love shiny objects."

Alice paid quickly for the few packs of sequins and tossed them in her purse. Then she asked Annie if she'd like to grab dinner at the diner.

"Is it that time already?" Annie said. "This day has flown by."

They walked out together, and Annie realized the sun had set while she was inside chatting with Mary Beth. The wind had picked up more and tossed Annie's fine blond hair.

Alice pushed her own auburn waves out of her face. "This time of year, I sometimes think Mary Beth has the right idea," she said. "The wind never blows that pixie cut she wears."

"It's the perfect look for Mary Beth," Annie said. "She looks like a nice elf mom. But I don't think it would suit either of us."

Alice pushed her hair aside again. "Probably not. But I think it's time to break out my scarf collection so I'm not trying to look through hair every time I go outside."

They had reached the door of The Cup & Saucer. As Annie pushed it open, she turned slightly to say, "I thought you just had all those scarves to look sporty in your convertible."

"Well, that too."

Peggy hurried over as soon as they came through the door. "I had so much fun yesterday," she said as she led them through the half-filled dining room. "Even if we didn't find anything mysterious, I now have the perfect outfit for the ball!"

"It looks great on you," Annie said as she slipped into the chair near the front window. This was her favorite table, at least until real winter set in. Then the cold coming off the glass made it a bit less pleasant. Now though, it offered a lovely view of the stores across the street with their warm light spilling out on the sidewalk and the streetlights glowing down in ambient puddles.

"I really recommend the sliced beef and gravy tonight," Peggy said. "The scent has been making my stomach growl ever since I came in."

"Sounds great," Alice said. "With coffee."

"Same for me," Annie agreed.

They chatted a bit about the upcoming ball and the fun they'd had in the attic. "I have to admit that I'm a little disappointed a nice, big mystery didn't jump out at us while we were in your attic," Alice said.

"That's because you're not the one who ends up with people upset with you every time we fall into a mystery," Annie said. "I'm perfectly happy just to look back on past mysteries and focus on fun now."

"Fun like going to the ball with Ian?" Alice teased, drawing Ian's name out.

"You know we're just friends."

Before Alice could reply, they were interrupted by Peggy with their dinners. The food looked as good as it smelled, and both women focused on their meals. Annie was just as glad to get off the topic of Ian. She still found her feelings for the handsome mayor confusing. She liked him. He was kind and attentive, but he wasn't Wayne. And she wasn't ready to consider anyone in her life who wasn't Wayne.

"You look serious," Alice said as she sipped her coffee. "What are you thinking about?"

"Wayne."

Alice nodded. "I wish I had met him. He must have been a great guy."

"He was," Annie said. "Of course, he was also a perfectly normal guy. Sometimes he made me crazy, and sometimes I made him crazy, but mostly we made each other happy."

"That must be nice," Alice said. "I had the crazy part with my ex, but I wouldn't mind a few years of happy."

"I thought you might be finding it with Jim a while back," Annie said.

Alice shook her head. "Jim makes me happy, but I don't think either of us could really see that relationship working. Jim is never in one place, and I've finally found exactly where I want to be." Then she grinned. "Not that I would mind if another staggeringly handsome guy wanted to waltz into my life and stay a while."

"Well, if one passes through Stony Point, I promise not to be any competition."

Alice's smile in reply suddenly froze on her face, and Annie felt a surge of alarm as Alice grew decidedly pale. Annie turned to see what Alice was looking at. In the doorway of the diner stood a tall, broad-shouldered man with perfectly trimmed black hair sprinkled with gray. The stranger looked around the room. When his eyes landed on Alice, his face lit up with a dazzlingly white smile.

"Do you know him?" Annie whispered.

Alice didn't answer, but she nodded slightly as the man crossed the room in a few quick strides. When he reached their table, he quickly bent to kiss Alice on the cheek. "You look beautiful," he said, his voice smooth and warm. Then he turned the full wattage of his smile toward Annie. "So Alice, are you going to introduce me to your friend?"

Alice seemed to shake off the trance she was in. "This is my best friend, Annie Dawson," she said. "Annie, this is my ex-husband, John MacFarlane."

Now it was Annie's turn to look stunned as the tall man reached out and took her hand, giving it a warm shake with a hand that sported a perfect manicure. Annie had to fight the urge to wipe her hand on her pants when John let go.

So this was the man who had broken Alice's heart. What could he possibly want now?

~5~

Annie fought the urge to fidget as John MacFarlane turned his warm smile back to Alice. She could see why Alice might have found him attractive when she was young. He looked like a movie star with his perfect white teeth and tanned complexion. Even the gray in his hair seemed almost artful, like he was trying to look mature and stable.

"What could possibly bring you to Stony Point?" Alice asked icily.

"After all the years you spent telling me how wonderful this town is," John said, raising an eyebrow slightly, "how could I not come and see for myself at least once?"

"You seemed able to resist the allure when we were married, and I wanted to come back home."

"I didn't want to share you then," he said.

"Right," Alice turned away and took a sip from her coffee cup. "As I remember, you didn't think I should feel the same way."

"Alice, I know I treated you terribly, but I'd like to make it up to you."

Now it was Alice's turn to raise an eyebrow. She didn't say anything, but just looked at him expectantly.

"I was hoping we could talk privately," he said.

Alice leaned toward him and said, "Then you shouldn't

have interrupted my dinner with a friend. I honestly cannot imagine anything you have to say that would interest me. I'm happy now, John. I don't need you anywhere near me."

The tall man stood straight and nodded. "I deserve that. I would still like to speak to you. I'm staying at Maplehurst Inn. Could I at least have five minutes of your time tomorrow?"

"I'll think about it and let you know." Alice turned very pointedly away from him and asked Annie if she'd chosen shoes to go with her ball gown.

"Um, no," Annie said nervously, trying to go along with Alice's pointed effort to ignore her ex. "I hadn't thought much about it. I have some ivory pumps that I think would go with it OK."

John MacFarlane stood beside them a moment. Then Peggy appeared at his side. "Are you joining this table, or do you need one of your own?" she asked.

"He needs one of his own," Alice said, and Peggy looked at her with her eyes full of curiosity.

He sighed. "I guess I need one of my own."

Peggy led him to a table as far from Annie and Alice as possible. Annie made a mental note to thank her later. Peggy could be a bit of a gossip sometimes, but her instincts about people were certainly first-rate.

"Well, I don't feel much like dessert," Alice said. "I think I'll head home."

Annie reached out and put her hand on Alice's arm. "Please, be careful if you do decide to talk to …" She let her voice trail off.

"Don't worry," Alice said. "If there is one thing I've

learned, it's to be very careful about John MacFarlane."
Then she forced a smile. "I'll be all right, really."

"Well, let me walk you out, at least," Annie said.

The women quickly paid their bill and left. Outside,
Alice leaned on a wall. "Give me a second," she said. "That
was one surprise I really didn't need."

"Are you all right?"

"I thought I was," Alice said, her smile forced. "But
don't worry. I'll be fine. I do think I'll pass on any more
chats with him."

Annie gave her friend a quick hug, and then Alice
straightened up. "Time to be a big girl. I'll talk to you later.
Thanks."

"I'm always available if you need to talk."

Alice nodded and the two walked to their cars.

Annie spent most of Friday working on her mask. Her
eyes often strayed in the direction of the carriage house, but
she didn't see Alice.

When Annie's mask was done, she stopped by the carriage house to see if Alice wanted to drive over to the inn
with her to drop off her mask too, since they were barely
making the deadline as it was—the auction was Saturday
afternoon. She didn't get an answer and finally had to go on
her own.

On Saturday morning, Annie looked over her gown for
the ball and mended a few weak seams. Then she draped
the delicate silk over her arm and grabbed her keys. She'd
take the dress to the cleaners, then she was going to quiz
Mary Beth to see if anyone had seen Alice. She was really
growing concerned about her friend.

As she walked out on the porch, she spotted Alice walking across the lawn, a sheepish look on her face and a wrapped basket in her hands. "Alice MacFarlane," Annie scolded, "I've been worried sick about you."

"I'm sorry," Alice said as she held up the basket. "I've brought a peace offering. Would you like some double-chocolate zucchini bread?"

"Double chocolate?" Annie said. "Sounds like comfort food."

Alice laughed a little. "And I can use it."

Annie turned and let Alice in the door, and then she draped the dress over the bench in the entry. "Come on in the kitchen," she said. "I have some fresh coffee to go with that bread."

Soon both women were seated with steaming cups of coffee and thick slabs of moist bread. "I finished my mask last night," Alice said. "Just in under the wire. In fact, I had to call so someone would stay an extra two hours to log it in yesterday. I've been distracted."

Annie nodded, waiting for Alice to get to the point. "So, I assume you decided to see your ex after all?"

Alice sipped her coffee, pausing before she nodded her head. "Yeah, I went to see John at the inn. He says cheating on me was the stupidest thing he ever did."

"I could agree with that," Annie said.

"Me too." Alice leaned back in her chair with a sigh. "He wants us to get back together. I told him that's never going to happen. He's not someone I want in my life any-more. I don't need that kind of turmoil, and I don't think I'd ever really trust him. That's no way to have a relationship."

"I agree with all that too," Annie said.

"I met him at the inn," Alice said. "So it was hard to avoid the topic of the ball and ..."

"Oh, Alice," Annie said. "You didn't."

Alice nodded. "I agreed to let John be my date for the ball. I want to keep an eye on him if he's going to be in town. Plus, it's my civic duty to keep the other women in Stony Point safe from John MacFarlane's charm."

"I'm not sure that's a good idea," Annie said slowly. "It feels like a terrible idea, in fact."

"Probably so," Alice said, "but I'm committed. You and Ian will be there and lots of other people I know. So it's not like I have to be alone with John that much. Honestly, I don't buy the whole bit about wanting to get back together. I think he's here for some other reason, and I guess I want to know why."

Annie shook her head worriedly. "I just don't want you to get hurt."

"I wish you'd caught me when I was twenty and just meeting him."

Silence fell over the kitchen with neither woman knowing just what to say next. Thankfully, it was broken when Boots padded in and began to demand attention. The conversation turned away from Alice's ex, and they chatted about the upcoming ball and mask auction.

"Do you want to go to the auction together?" Alice asked. "Could be fun."

Annie readily agreed. They chatted only a few more minutes before Alice left, making plans for Annie to drive them to the auction later. Annie felt better now that she'd seen Alice, but she was still worried. John MacFarlane was certainly handsome and charming. He and Alice shared a history, and she hoped her friend would tread carefully.

Once again, Annie felt a surge of gratitude for her own life. She missed Wayne fiercely, but at least her memories of their time together were full of trust and love. She'd never once doubted his faithfulness. He never gave her reason to doubt him.

Just before time for the auction, Annie pulled the car down to Alice's driveway so her friend wouldn't have to wade through leaves. Alice was walking down the porch steps of the carriage house, and Annie waved brightly at her as she rolled to a stop. She was pleased to see Alice looked cheery—clearly she wasn't brooding about John. Alice had changed into a gorgeous, olive green military-style jacket that set off her auburn hair, making it almost look like flame. The shell she wore under the jacket and her slacks matched her hair color almost exactly.

"You look great," Annie said as Alice slipped into the car. "I wish I could pull off some of those colors."

"Autumn is my season," Alice said. "Plus, I always try to wear unusual colors to an auction. They draw the auctioneer's eye. That can make a difference in tight bidding."

Annie laughed. "I don't picture this mask auction turning into the competition of the century."

"You never know. I believe in being prepared."

Annie noticed her friend tensed up slightly as they pulled in at Maplehurst Inn. "I just hope we don't run into John," Alice said.

"I'll keep my fingers crossed," Annie said. "I need to

stop at the dry cleaners on the way to the auction and drop my gown off for cleaning."

After Annie left her gown at the dry cleaners, the friends proceeded to Maplehurst Inn. As they entered the inn, they found rows of tables with flat glass cases laid out on them throughout the inn's lobby area. At one end of the row, a desk had been set up for the auction participants to register and get a paddle with a number on it for bidding.

Annie saw Liz Booth standing behind the registration table talking to a tall, elegant woman who looked to be in her early thirties. Annie didn't recognize her. Alice tugged on Annie's arm and drew her attention to the nearest glass case. "Look at that mask," Alice said. "It's gorgeous."

Annie had to agree. The mask form had been spray-painted a smooth metallic silver. Then a delicate butterfly design in gold leaf covered much of the silver. From the left side of the mask, metal filigree leaf shapes in gold and silver curved up and over the left side of the mask's forehead. Gold and silver wire in varying widths wove around the stick the mask wearer would hold.

"Wow," Annie said. "I can't imagine making something like that. Clearly some people heard about this mask auction a long time before we did."

Alice nodded. "Not that I could have made some of these even if you'd given me a year or two."

As they continued peeking into the cases, they saw at least a dozen masks with the kind of expensive look of that first mask. One mask was done in delicate gold filigree with sparkling jewel highlights that Annie certainly hoped were just rhinestones.

"They're certainly beautiful, but I can't imagine carrying something quite that elaborate with my gown," Annie said. "I hope they have some simpler designs."

Soon they came to a few cases with masks that looked a bit more in Annie's price range. As they walked, they passed the doorway to the ballroom, and Alice tugged Annie's arm again. "We'd better register and go inside," she said. "We'll never get a good seat if we look at all the masks first."

Annie nodded and they walked over to the registration table. Liz and the young woman still stood behind the table, talking intently, but Liz stopped and smiled as they walked up. "Hello Annie, Alice," she said. "I'd like you ladies to meet Mrs. Victoria Meyer. She's sponsoring the auction."

"How do you do." Annie said warmly.

The young woman responded politely, but with a flatness in her voice that suggested she had little interest in further conversation.

"Why did you pick Alzheimer's research as the charity?" Alice asked curiously.

"A close member of my family suffered from the disease," Mrs. Meyer said simply and a bit dismissively. She was certainly not a person who invited further chat.

As Alice bent over to fill out her registration form, Annie studied Mrs. Meyer quietly. The young woman's black dress was cut simply, but Annie could tell it was expensive. It fit perfectly, and the design suited the tall, cool woman, setting off her fair skin and light wintry blue eyes. The young woman's blond hair would have been a perfect match in color to Annie's own, minus the few gray streaks that Annie's grandchildren called her "sparkles."

As if sensing eyes on her, the woman turned to look coolly over Annie's own gray-blue wool skirt and matching sweater. The slight cold smile she offered oozed superiority, and Annie found a strong dislike rising up in her. She didn't normally dislike people on sight, but Mrs. Meyer definitely didn't seem very friendly or appealing.

Alice tapped Annie's arm, handing her the pen, and she quickly registered and received her auction paddle. "Good luck with the auction," Alice said as they backed away from the table.

"Thanks," Liz replied. The cool blonde beside her didn't say anything at all.

"Whew," Alice said as she and Annie went into the ballroom. "Nice to get out of the chill. I do believe that girl could out-snooty Stella."

Annie smiled at the idea of a showdown as they looked around the room for seats. She spotted a number of people she recognized amongst the rapidly filling seats. Most of the rows at the center left of the room were roped off with "reserved" signs hanging from the rope. A few very well-dressed women already sat in that section. Annie saw Gwen Palmer standing outside the roped-in area and chatting with the older women seated inside.

"Wow, they must be quite a bunch if Gwen has to be on the outside," Alice said.

Annie didn't answer. She was beginning to wonder if she'd made a mistake agreeing to go to the ball with Ian. Certainly, if it was going to be an event with a clear divide between people based on money, she'd really rather not go.

Liz Booth passed through the crowd and took a place at

the front of the room. The microphone in front of her crack-led as she adjusted it. "Can everyone take a seat, please?"

After a quick scurrying as those standing found seats, Liz smiled at someone behind them, and a young man in a Maplehurst Inn waiter uniform carried up a lovely ball mask. The mask form was covered in smooth white bro-cade, and a beaded fleur-de-lis was centered on the fore-head. Where the stick joined the corner of the mask, loops of glass beads accented the temple. "This mask was donat-ed by the Hook and Needle Club here in Stony Point," Liz said, and Annie felt a twinge of curiosity about which of her friends had created the lovely piece. Since she didn't see any sequins, she assumed it wasn't Alice's mask. "Opening bids on all masks begin at twenty dollars. Can I get twenty for this lovely piece that is certain to complement many dif-ferent gowns?"

Annie glanced around and saw paddles raise here and there for a few minutes as the bidding crept up, and then everyone was still. The lovely white mask sold for forty dol-lars. Annie breathed a sigh of relief. Clearly some of the masks would be within her price range.

Several more pretty masks came up, donated by differ-ent civic groups and businesses around Stony Point. Bids continued to stay in a comfortable range, but Annie started to worry about finding something that would actually go with her dress. She suspected the bright sparkly masks would quickly overwhelm her simple gown. Then she brightened as Liz said, "We have another donation from the Hook and Needle Club." The waiter held up a mask covered in deli-cate, ivory crocheted flowers on a smooth green satin base.

The flowers were a masterpiece of crochet artistry, and Annie quickly put her paddle up when bidding began.

Again she looked around and saw only a couple others were bidding on the same mask, but those bidding seemed to really want it. Paddles flashed as Liz raised the bid again and again. Annie bit her lip and raised her paddle to signal a bid of seventy dollars. "I can't go much higher," she whispered to Alice as she looked at the two other bidders who had hung in so far. One twitched her paddle a bit but didn't raise it. Annie had won!

"Sold for seventy dollars," Liz said.

"It's going to be perfect with your dress," Alice whispered. "Kate had to have made that one. I don't know anyone else who could crochet those tiny flowers with that kind of detail."

Annie nodded. The mask was a little treasure, and Annie decided she'd hang it on the wall somewhere after the ball. After Kate's mask, the next piece to come up was the gold mask studded with gemstones that Annie had seen in the case outside.

"This next mask was donated by the Forsythe family," Liz said. "It was designed by Palermo Vanzetti."

Alice gasped, and Annie turned to look at her. "You don't recognize that name?" Alice asked.

Annie shook her head.

"He's a major jewelry designer to the ultra rich," Alice said. "How did they get him to do a mask for a dinky auction like this?"

Annie shook her head as bidding went on fast and furious around her. Soon though, it became too high for anyone outside the reserved seats. When the last paddle dropped, the mask had sold to a distinguished man in a handsome charcoal suit for fifteen thousand dollars.

"I would hate to be the mask that follows that," Alice whispered, fanning herself with her paddle.

That's when Liz said, "We have another donation from the Hook and Needle Club here in Stony Point." Annie's eyes jumped to the front and she recognized her own mask and nearly groaned. She figured she'd be lucky to get one bid when people compared her shabby little mask to the jeweled masterpiece that had just sold.

"Oh, nice," Alice said as she raised her paddle. Annie figured Alice must have recognized the pieces she'd cannibalized from the attic and was offering a mercy bid. But then several other bids came in quickly.

Annie smiled in relief as the bidding quickly reached fifty dollars with Alice clearly committed to getting the mask. Suddenly a voice rang out from the back of the room. "One thousand dollars."

Annie and Alice turned in shock. Victoria Meyer stood at the back of the room. She didn't even have a paddle. Liz blinked a moment, but then went smoothly on. "The bid is one thousand dollars," she said. "Can I get one thousand and twenty?"

No one moved in the audience, and the mask was sold to Victoria.

"Wow," Alice said. "I guess she *really* wanted it. That solves the question of which of the Hook and Needle masks sells for the most. That one!"

"I guess," Annie said vaguely. But she was completely

confused. Why would someone bid that kind of money for her simple mask?

The rest of the auction passed in a bit of a blur. Alice managed to buy a lovely mask that had been donated by Dress to Impress, a cute shop across the street from The Cup & Saucer.

"I'm so glad I'll be wearing Kate's mask to the ball," Annie said as they joined the folks heading out of the ballroom. "She's done so much to help me with my own work, but I can't imagine ever being the artist that Kate is."

"I wouldn't say never," Alice answered. "You've taken on some tough projects."

Annie laughed. "Taken on isn't the same as accomplished. I can hardly wait for the next Hook and Needle Club meeting so Kate can help me fix the mess I'm making of my sweater."

"You're always too hard on yourself."

A voice interrupted the two friends. "Excuse me."

Annie and Alice turned to see Victoria Meyer standing behind them with a warm smile on her face. "Aren't you Annie Dawson?" the young woman said. "I believe you made the mask I bought."

"I did," Annie said, startled by the change in Victoria. She looked so friendly and interested as her smile grew bigger.

"I'm so glad to meet you," Victoria said. "I just love my mask. How did you make it?"

"I'm afraid it's a scraps project," Annie admitted. "I used fabric from my grandmother's scraps basket and broken jewelry I found in the attic."

"Oh, I did wonder if that lovely emerald piece was originally from an earring," Victoria said. "It's a unique piece and exquisitely made."

"I'm certain it's just costume jewelry," Annie said, hoping the young woman hadn't paid so much because she thought the mask had a real emerald on it.

"Oh, I know," Victoria said with a sparkling laugh. "It's the design that interests me more than the value. I love that tree motif. Did you find other pieces in the set?"

"How did you know it was a set?" Alice cut in.

"Well, earrings do come in pairs, don't they?" Victoria said, her voice turning a bit cooler as she turned her attention to Alice.

"I have the second earring if you want it," Annie said. "Do you want me to bring it by here?"

"Oh, you're so kind," the young woman said, her smile warm again. "Is that all you have? Just the earrings?"

Suddenly, the harried young man manning the table called for the next person in line. Annie excused herself and went to pay for her mask. She was pleased to see it was every bit as lovely up close as she'd hoped.

She turned to show it to Alice and was surprised to see Victoria still stood there, clearly wanting to talk more.

"Kate did an amazing job," Alice said. "You're going to look fantastic." Then Alice ducked around Victoria so she could reach the table and pay for her mask.

"That is a very nice piece," Victoria said, her eyes barely flitting to the mask. "Though I do like the one you made better. Maybe I could come by your house to get the second earring?"

"That won't be necessary," Annie said. "I can bring it to you."

"Oh, I don't mind. I could maybe wear it in my hair at the ball to match the one on the mask. I do love unique jewelry."

"Victoria?"

"What?" Victoria's response almost snapped as she turned to face Liz Booth, who had interrupted to ask her something about the auction. While Victoria's attention was turned away, Annie slipped outside. She'd had enough of the moody young woman's behavior. Wealth seemed no excuse for poor manners.

Annie stood a few moments on the front steps of Maplehurst Inn and smiled when she saw a gust of wind send crispy leaves dancing in the driveway. A few minutes later, Alice came out of the inn to join her. "So this is where you disappeared to," Alice said. "That Meyer person practically demanded to know where you were."

"She is a bit aggressive," Annie said. "I wonder why she's so interested in that jewelry. You don't think those gems could be real?"

"No, I looked them over," Alice said. "They're nice costume jewelry, but those aren't real gems." She grinned mischievously. "Trust me, I know jewelry. The whole set might be worth a couple hundred dollars, through. It is nice stuff."

"I don't think a couple hundred dollars would impress that young woman much."

"No. Her shoes cost way more than that," Alice said, dropping her voice to a whisper. "Did you see them? I'm absolutely certain they were Roger Vivier."

"Which are?"

"French and definitely worth more than all the jewelry in your attic combined."

Annie sighed. "Well, maybe she was just trying to be friendly. I don't want to start seeing mysteries where they don't exist."

─6─

Annie spent the rest of the day half expecting Victoria Meyer to show up on her doorstep, demanding to root through all her costume jewelry. She was pleased when nothing unusual happened.

"Well, perhaps asking questions is her way of being friendly," she said to Boots, who showed her extreme disinterest by yawning widely.

"You're right," Annie agreed. "I have better things to think about. Like making sure I'm ready for the ball next Saturday!"

Still, in case the woman really did want the second earring, the next morning Annie dropped it off at the desk at Maplehurst Inn.

The weather turned rainy by Sunday afternoon, and Annie stayed close to home, working on her sweater. Boots clearly found the soft, fuzzy green yarn as attractive as Annie did, as Annie twice had to catch the cat in the midst of yarn theft.

"I still haven't found the last ball you stole," Annie said, scolding the cat while she cuddled her. "I bought you a nice ball with a bell in it. Why don't you go find that and play with it?"

Boots just purred in response. The ringing phone interrupted Annie's failed attempt at cat discipline, so

Annie carried the cat with her to the phone. It was Annie's daughter, LeeAnn.

"Oh, please tell me you're calling to finalize your plan to come for Thanksgiving," Annie said, tucking the phone into her shoulder as she set the cat on the floor.

"Mom," LeeAnn said, "remember all the times you scolded me for nagging you about moving back to Texas?"

"That just means I've earned some free nagging back at you."

LeeAnn moaned. "Well, that is *not* what I'm calling about. I just had to tell you what costume Joanna decided on for Halloween."

Annie sat down in the chair beside the phone and curled her legs under her. "What costume?"

"She wants to go as twins," LeeAnn said.

"She wants matching costumes with John?"

"No, not twins with her real twin. She wants to be twins with the doll you gave her for her birthday. So, I was hoping you might have some of the fabric you used for the costume?"

Annie laughed. "The apron was just muslin, but I found the calico in Gram's fabric collection. There's definitely more of it. I don't know if there's enough for a dress to fit Joanna. Are she and her brother still growing like weeds?"

"Wild weeds," LeeAnn said. "Can you overnight the fabric? I really need to get going on the costume if I'm going to get it done in time. Thankfully, John wants to be a boat captain; he has most of that stuff in their dress-up box."

Just as Annie was about to answer, Boots raced by her with a bundle of green in her mouth. "Boots!" Annie yelped.

Then she told LeeAnn that she had to go. A yarn-napping was happening right in front of her.

"No problem," LeeAnn said. "I need to run anyway. Don't forget about the fabric."

"I won't," Annie promised. She hung up and hurried into the kitchen where she'd seen the cat run. Looking around, she couldn't find Boots. Then she remembered the time the cat had dragged a doll into the crack between the end of the cabinets and the wall. "I've got to get Wally to fix that."

She dug the flashlight out of the junk drawer and shone the light into the crack. No cat and no yarn ball. Puzzled, Annie headed into the mudroom. She used the flashlight to look under the benches where several pairs of rain boots lay scattered. That's when she spotted the cat huddled over the yarn ball.

"You're turning into a terrible crook," Annie said as she took the yarn from the disgruntled cat. Then she had an idea. She flashed the light into each of the overturned boots. Inside she found Boots's bell ball, the missing ball of yarn, a leftover piece of black ribbon from Annie's mask project, and something else fuzzy wadded deep in the toe.

Annie shook the boot upside down and the matted fuzzy thing fell out on the floor. It was a dead mouse. Annie shrieked and leapt to her feet. Boots nabbed the dead mouse and made a run for the kitchen. This time the cat did duck into the crack between the counter and wall.

Shuddering slightly, Annie carried her yarn to the front room, stuffed it into her project bag, and put the bag far out of the cat's reach. She tossed the bell ball into the middle of the room. The bell jingled but no cat appeared.

Annie walked back into the kitchen and opened a can of tuna. Like magic the cat appeared at her ankles. "Forget it," Annie said. "I'm not rewarding you for being so naughty. I guess I'm going to have tuna salad for lunch." She put a bowl over the open can of tuna and then used the broom to fish the dead mouse out of the crack and dispose of it outside.

After the mouse eradication, Annie quickly packaged up the fabric LeeAnn had asked for and added a note telling her how the story of the yarn napping had ended. "I solved the mystery of the stolen yarn," she wrote. "As far as I'm concerned, I'm ready to live mystery-free now."

Not that Annie ever got to be mystery free for long.

～7～

y Tuesday, Annie was really looking forward to the meeting of the Hook and Needle Club as her sweater project was as far along as she could manage on her own. Although she'd finished the cables on the front of the sweater, somehow the one that ran down the arm of each sweater sleeve had her baffled. The stitch was slightly different, and Annie just couldn't wrap her mind around it somehow. Finally, she stuffed it into her project bag and hoped Kate could save her.

The weather turned warmer with the end of the rain, as if not wanting to leave summer totally behind, and Tuesday was bright and cool. A brisk rain had driven many of the leaves off the trees, but Annie tried not to look at them as she hurried out to her car. "They need a couple days to dry before I can rake them," she told herself.

She stopped at the cleaners on the way to the meeting to pick up her dress. She so hoped the delicate dress had survived the cleaning process, but the results more than delighted her. The cleaners had done a wonderful job with it, and the soft colors now almost seemed to glow. Annie was relieved to see the old fabric showed no signs of damage.

She laid the dress carefully across the backseat before hurrying to A Stitch in Time. As usual, the chairs were full when she got there, and everyone was talking about the auction. Though Stella's needles worked steadily on her project, everyone else was caught up in auction fever.

"Alice said you bought the mask I made," Kate said. "I was so afraid no one would want it."

"Plenty of people wanted it," Alice said. "There was practically a bidding war. Annie had to fight tooth and nail for it."

Annie laughed. "I don't know about that, but bidding did go quite high. I was lucky to win. It's absolutely perfect for my gown."

"Speaking of bidding wars," Gwen said. "You clearly won our little challenge, hands down, Annie. I couldn't believe it when Victoria bid a thousand dollars to get your mask."

At that, Annie was bombarded by questions by those who hadn't been at the auction. She really didn't have many answers. She had no idea why the wealthy young woman had wanted her mask so much or bid so highly.

"As long as it's for a good cause, I don't suppose it really matters," Stella said.

"You're right," Annie said, but she couldn't help wondering.

The rest of the week passed all too quickly as Annie fretted about the ball. She knew it was silly to worry so much, but she wanted to look good for Ian. It wasn't about romance, she told herself firmly several times. It was simply a matter of not wanting the mayor to look bad.

She had bought new shoes after looking over her collection of comfy slip-ons. She had even considered getting the "sparkles" in her hair covered, but quickly rejected the idea. She had earned the strands of gray with a lovely lifetime,

and her grandchildren loved them. That was good enough
for her.

By the time Saturday rolled around, Annie felt she had
everything under control. Then she tried to fix her hair.
Normally Annie wore her hair one of two ways: up in a short
ponytail when she was working in the garden or cleaning
house, or long and loose. But a ball seemed to call for something a little more elaborate. She tried a variety of different
hairdos, some requiring a lot more hairspray than she usually went for, but nothing seemed quite right, and time was
ticking away.

In desperation, she hurried off to take a shower so she
could start over. After a quick blow-dry, she slipped into her
gown. The fabric fluttered lightly around her ankles, and
Annie smiled at her image in the mirror. *Well, at least I have
a great dress,* she thought as she pushed her stocking-clad
feet into her ivory heels. Since she hadn't really dressed up
in years, the shoes felt a little strange and wobbly.

The feeling brought back a memory of a long-ago formal
dance and the first time she'd worn really high heels since
her high school prom. When Wayne had come to pick her
up, he seemed almost awestruck at the sight of her. She
smiled as she thought of how he'd fumbled with the cor-
sage, having no idea how to pin it to her strapless gown.
She'd eventually rescued him and pinned it on herself.

Then he'd practically galloped to the car, all his nerves
coming out in that long-legged dash. There was no way she
could keep up in the high heels. She'd wobbled down the
front walk, feeling abandoned. Finally, she'd stopped and
put her hands on her hips, completely annoyed.

At the car, he'd opened the door, and then he turned to find she was only halfway down the walk. "Is something wrong?"

"You should have told me this was a sprint," she'd said. "I would have worn track shoes."

He'd flushed so pink she could see it even in the dim light from the porch. He'd hurried back and offered his arm. And for the rest of the evening, he'd hovered over her as if she might fall down at any moment and need carrying. In his own way, he'd stayed right by her side from then on, just in case she needed him.

Annie blinked as her image blurred in the mirror. Her life was blessed now in so many ways with good friends here in Stony Point, but how dearly she missed the security of Wayne by her side.

Annie took a deep breath and turned away from the mirror to root through Gram's jewelry box for the fine strand of seed pearls she knew was in there. She quickly slipped them on and added the small diamond earrings that were her most valuable jewels.

A glance at the clock made her yelp. Ian would be there soon, and she still didn't know what to do with her hair. Maybe something simple? She twisted her hair into a chignon and looked around on her dresser top for something she could use to hold the hair in place. Then she remembered the hair comb from the emerald set.

Annie kicked off her shoes for speed and hurried downstairs to the living room where she'd left the jewelry box with her mask-making supplies. She carried the box back to her bedroom and twisted her hair again, using the comb to secure it. A few fine wisps of hair floated down, but somehow the comb made it look artful, not messy. Annie gave it a quick spritz of hair spray and hoped for the best.

Boots had watched most of her preparations from a place of comfort, sprawled on the bed, but as Annie turned she found the gray cat batting at the sparkling necklace in the jewelry box. "I don't think so," she scolded.

She closed the box and shoved it under the pillows to keep Boots from getting back into it. The sound of the doorbell startled her. "I guess it's showtime," she said, taking a deep breath and slipping back into her shoes.

She opened the front door just as Ian pressed the doorbell again. "Sorry to keep you waiting," Annie said as she opened the door and stepped back. She noticed how well the black tuxedo set off Ian's long-legged figure. "I'm about ready. Let me just get my mask."

"I don't mind waiting," Ian answered as he stepped in. "If you'll forgive the cliché, you're worth it."

"You know Gram always told me to beware of charming men," Annie said.

Ian raised one eyebrow. "From what I've heard, your grandfather was very charming."

"There's an exception to every rule." Annie picked up the floral-trimmed mask and held it in front of her face. "What do you think?"

"That's a beautiful mask," Ian said. "Kate's work?"

"Yes. Isn't it beautiful?" Annie replied. "It went for a higher selling price than I had expected, but I just had to have it! I didn't see you at the auction; do you have a mask?"

"I ordered mine online to match this penguin suit I'm

wearing." He opened his tuxedo jacket and reached into an inner pocket to pull out a white ceramic mask with a black stripe down the center and a beak. Somehow it managed to be very whimsical and classy at the same time. It had a band to hold it on, and Ian slipped it over his head.

Annie burst into laughter. "I'm seeing a whole different side of you, Mr. Mayor."

Boots had followed Annie downstairs to flop on the sofa. When Annie laughed, the cat raised her head to give Annie a grumpy meow. Boots took one look at Ian in his pointy-nosed mask and raced out of the room. Annie and Ian left together, still laughing at the temperamental cat.

Ian had left his truck at home, and Annie was glad. She settled into the smooth seat of his car and enjoyed being surrounded by the scent of the leather. In the hot summer, she appreciated the fabric seats in her Malibu, but on a cool evening there was something luxurious about being in a long, silk gown and nestled in a leather seat.

The drive to Maplehurst Inn was short, and they soon pulled up in front of the inn. For the night of the ball, the Historical Society had hired some of the local teens to park cars in order to get the most people into their small parking lot and into the overflow parking they were borrowing from the Stony Point Cultural Center.

Annie didn't mind; it meant less walking on uneven ground in her heels. Ian opened her door and offered his hand as she climbed out. Then he tossed the keys to the grinning teenager before tucking Annie's hand into the crook of his arm and walking up the walk toward the inn's wide front porch.

"You're very suave tonight, Mr. Mayor," Annie said with a smile.

Ian laughed. "It must be the tux."

As they walked up the steps to the porch, Annie noticed the mums lining the whole length of the porch rails. "They definitely look better on this porch than on mine."

"This porch is bigger, though they certainly added a unique touch to your house."

"It made me look like a flower hoarder," she said.

They walked through the front door and handed their tickets to a young woman who stood there in a Maplehurst waitstaff uniform. "Have a lovely evening," she said, smiling.

The lobby of the inn had been transformed again. All the tables that had held the masks for the auction were gone. Now the space was mostly empty with cozy couches and chairs lining the walls. Music drifted from the main ballroom that served as a formal dining room for the inn most of the time. As Annie looked through the open French doors she saw most of the white-draped tables were gone and a small stage now stood at one end of the long room. A band played extremely golden oldies.

Ian touched Annie's arm, and her attention turned back to the foyer where they stood. Her eyes drifted over the couples scattered throughout the room. She spotted Peggy and Wally chatting with two people Annie didn't immediately recognize. Peggy caught Annie's glance, and her face lit up. She practically dragged Wally across the room.

Annie had to admit her friend looked lovely. In her waitress uniform, Peggy always looked pretty and plump, but tonight she looked voluptuous and glamorous in a very Marilyn Monroe way. The red gown hugged her curves, and though it covered her modestly enough, there was something daring about the style and color.

Peggy's black hair was swept back from her face in a sleek up-do, though the length in the back hung in loose curls.

"You look gorgeous," Annie said.

"I agree," Ian said. "And your tuxedo is considerably less ridiculous than mine, Wally."

Wally reached up to tug at his collar until Peggy pulled his hand away. "Mine feels silly enough," he said, then turned to Annie. "But I do appreciate the loan of it. All this has made Peggy very happy."

"I love that hair comb on you," Peggy said. "I think Alice was right. All those emeralds look good with your eyes."

"Mostly it saved me from total hair horror."

The other couple that Peggy and Wally had been speaking with drifted over now, and Annie smiled at them, finally recognizing Ian's brother Todd.

"Annie," Ian said. "You know my brother Todd and his wife Elizabeth."

Annie nodded, although Todd looked very different in the elegant dinner jacket and crisply pressed slacks he wore compared with his normal rugged fishing gear. As polite greetings were exchanged, Annie looked for signs of family resemblance between Ian and Todd. Todd was shorter and stockier. His shoulders and biceps clearly strained the fabric of his satin dinner jacket.

After the first exchange of pleasantries, Todd suddenly

stiffened and looked toward the front door. "What are those two doing here?"

Ian and Annie turned to look. She recognized the bouncy young scientist she'd met at A Stitch in Time. She and the man beside her were dressed in Victorian-style explorer costumes.

"I suppose they bought a ticket like everyone else," Ian said mildly.

Todd just grumbled until his wife finally tugged him away toward a low table covered in canopy trays. She was just in time, because Jenna Paige had spotted Annie and Peggy, and was towing her date across the room toward them.

"Oh, I'm so glad to see friends!" Jenna gushed when she reached them.

"It's nice to see you again," Annie said. She turned to Ian. "Have you met Dr. Paige?"

"I don't believe I have." Ian bowed slightly. "I'm Ian Butler, mayor of Stony Point."

"Oh, the mayor! That must be so exciting! Are you two married?"

Annie blinked. "No, we're just friends."

"Oh, that's exactly like Simon and me," she said. "We're just super friends." Then she giggled. "But we're not *the* Super Friends, of course. Though I would love to be Wonder Woman. Wouldn't that be fun?"

Peggy gently interrupted the gush and introduced her husband. Then Jenna introduced them to Dr. Simon Gunderson, a slightly balding young man who looked around with a distracted frown.

"So are you both enjoying your work in Stony Point?" Ian asked.

"It's fairly routine," Simon Gunderson said quietly, with a decidedly Southern accent. "But I find the town fascinating. As mayor, I'm sure you know a great deal about it—the history and such."

"Not as much as the Historical Society," Ian said. "But my family has lived here for many generations."

"Excellent," the young man's vague look sharpened. "I actually have a number of questions."

Annie expected the biologist to launch into a series of questions about fishing, but instead he asked about how the town government was structured and various things about the town's families.

Annie's attention was drawn by Jenna Paige's hand on her arm. "I love your hair comb," she gushed. "It's just beautiful. I am wild about emeralds. Not that I have any, but they're just so beautiful. Did you know they're actually much rarer than diamonds? The value of diamonds is kept artificially high by careful management by diamond cartels. They're not really nearly as rare as most people think. You can count on emeralds though. They'll never lose their value because they're truly rare."

"Oh," Annie said. "Isn't that interesting."

Peggy smiled mischievously. "Well, I guess we shouldn't sink our millions into diamonds then."

Jenna looked at her with a completely serious face. "That's wise. Emeralds are a much wiser investment. You should do like your friend."

Annie was about to explain that the emeralds in the

hair comb were fake when Ian gently took her arm. "I'm going to ask you to excuse us," Ian said. "As mayor, I do need to mingle a bit, and I'm going to have to drag Annie away with me."

Jenna giggled. "Of course; see you later, Annie!"

Ian led her toward the ballroom door. Annie looked at him with a slight smile. "Was Dr. Gunderson wearing on you?"

"Probably no more than Dr. Paige was on you," he said. "I will need to keep an eye on them though. Elizabeth is amazingly good at calming my brother, but he has a pretty big head of steam up about this lobster count, and we don't need any shouting matches at this ball."

They walked through the doors into the ballroom, and Annie gasped. The room was nearly full of couples. Some were dancing, the vintage costumes and masks looking elegant and otherworldly on the dance floor. Others stood along the sides of the room, chatting in small groups.

That's when Annie spotted Victoria Meyer. The tall woman looked as haughty as Annie remembered. She wore a gold gown that poured over her figure like a fabric fountain. Then Annie spotted the ornately jeweled mask in Mrs. Meyer's hand and realized the man standing beside her was the one who had bought the elaborate mask at the auction. Annie's face darkened in a puzzled frown. Why did the young woman pay such a ridiculous amount for the mask Annie made if she wasn't going to wear it to the ball?

— 8 —

As Annie looked over the other woman's ball gown, she realized her mask would never have gone with it. The golden mask studded with jewels was a perfect match. Then Annie gave a small mental shrug. Maybe the young woman had changed gowns when her husband gave her the gift of the jeweled mask.

Just then, Mrs. Meyer turned to look fully at Annie. A sudden flash of surprise crossed the young woman's face.

Someone stepped into Annie's line of sight, pulling her back into the moment. Mackenzie stood in front of her with her arm linked through Vanessa's arm. Annie was surprised to see Vanessa looking glum.

"Hi girls," Ian said. "You both look lovely."

"Your mother did a fantastic job on that gown, Vanessa," Annie added.

The delicate crocheted gown sparkled from the fine ice blue silk yarn that was twisted with thin silver strands. Vanessa managed to smile a little. "Thanks, Mrs. Dawson," she said. "Mom worked like crazy to get it done in time. She made my mask too."

Vanessa held up the mask on the stick and Annie saw it was a lacy crochet done in the same yarn as the 1920s-style dress, and then made hard with fabric stiffener to hold its shape. "I see you bought Mom's other mask," Vanessa said.

"She made zillions of those little flowers when I was a kid. She sewed them on all my clothes when I was little to fancy them up."

"The kids started calling her 'Daisy,'" Mackenzie said, and then she smiled. "But in the nicest way."

"She says that because *she's* one of the ones who started it," Vanessa said, throwing a mock scowl at her friend. "I asked Mom to stop putting flowers on my clothes, so I'm glad she finally found a place to put them."

"I'm glad too," Annie said. "They're lovely."

Vanessa nodded; then her eyes swept the room, and Annie saw her frown again.

"I thought you were looking forward to the ball," Annie said quietly. "You seem a little down."

Vanessa pointed through the crowd. "Because of *that!*"

Annie followed her line of vision and saw Vanessa's father, Harry Stevens. He stood near a blond woman quite a bit younger than himself. In fact, Annie suspected the woman was barely into her twenties. The young woman wore a ridiculously tight, slinky dress that stopped well above her knees. The dress didn't look even slightly "vintage."

"Oh," Annie said.

Ian frowned slightly. "Well, your parents *are* divorced, Vanessa."

"I know," Vanessa said. "And I know they can date other people. I'm *not* a kid. But she's so … so …" Her voice trailed off, and she just glared instead of finishing.

Annie had to agree. The young woman really was something else.

Right about then, Harry seemed to catch sight of

Vanessa. He wove through the crowd toward her with the blonde leaning so heavily on his arm that he listed slightly to one side.

"Hi, baby," he said when he reached them. He leaned over to give Vanessa a kiss on the cheek. She didn't pull away, but she did frown at her father's date. "You haven't met my friend, Sunny!"

"Pleased to meet you, kid," Sunny said.

"How do you do?" Vanessa replied stiffly.

"I do just fine," Sunny said, and then giggled close to Harry's ear. "Don't I, Harry?"

Harry glared at her. "This is my kid, Sunny!"

"She's a big girl," Sunny said with a shrug. Then she turned to look pointedly at Ian and Annie, but Harry didn't offer to introduce them. Sunny leaned closer to Annie. "That's a pretty hair comb. I love sparkly things."

"Like a crow," Vanessa muttered quietly, bringing a frown from her father.

"Maybe I could borrow it sometime?" Sunny said, apparently not hearing Vanessa's remark.

Annie looked at her in surprise. She didn't know how to respond to a perfect stranger wanting to borrow her things, but she was rescued by Ian who asked Harry where he had met Sunny. Instead of letting Harry answer, Sunny spoke up. "I'm a waitress in Storm Harbor," she said. "Harry's my favorite customer."

Annie could see Vanessa readying another remark, but this time Mackenzie cut in. "I'm going to drag Vanessa out to find some food and show off our gowns. Nice meeting you, Sunny." Then she pulled her friend toward the door while Vanessa glared daggers at Sunny.

With his daughter gone, it was clear Harry had no urge to continue any conversation with Annie and Ian. An awkward pause settled on them until Sunny announced that she was ready to dance, and they moved away through the crowd.

Ian grinned down at Annie. "Your hair comb has been quite a hit tonight." He tilted his head as he looked at it. "It *is* pretty. Was it Betsy's?"

"I don't think so," Annie said. "It's not really Gram's style. Or mine for that matter. But it's a pretty thing. I found the set in the attic."

"Ah, the mysterious attic."

Annie laughed lightly. "So far the attic hasn't been nearly as mysterious and full of conflict as this masquerade ball."

Ian looked over the crowd and raised an eyebrow. "Oh? Looks normal enough to me—maybe a little fancy."

"But we have the mystery of the chattering biologists," Annie said.

The corner of Ian's mouth turned up slightly. "They do like to talk."

"And ask questions," Annie said. "But none of the questions are about fishing or lobsters or anything you'd expect of a biologist."

"Astute observation, Detective Dawson," Ian teased.

"And there's the mystery of the changing masks." Annie explained about Mrs. Meyer paying such a large amount for Annie's mask and then carrying a totally different mask.

"I have a theory," Ian said. "Perhaps her husband bought the gold mask at the auction as a gift. Since he paid a lot more for it, naturally she'd bring that one."

"That is an excellent hypothesis, Detective Butler. But we have another perplexing mystery."

Ian raised his eyebrows quizzically and Annie said, "The mystery of what Harry sees in that young woman."

This brought a full-out laugh from Ian. "That is far too obvious to be a mystery."

As they talked, Annie's eyes continued to move over the crowd. Finally she stopped and nodded. "And there's the biggest mystery of all. What has brought John MacFarlane to Stony Point?"

Ian looked up in surprise. Alice and John stood some distance away, talking seriously. "Now that *is* a mystery. Maybe we should go and greet them, Detective Dawson."

"Excellent idea, Detective Butler."

Annie and Ian crossed the room, pausing several times as different people called out to the mayor. Twice they had to stop and exchange short conversations with people Ian knew. Anytime he introduced Annie, she caught very interested looks and more than one knowing—or was it assuming?—smile.

It was a relief to reach Alice and John. They stood in a small alcove at one side of the ballroom, and Annie's and Ian's arrival broke up some kind of serious discussion. Annie noticed that Alice greeted them with real relief. She quickly introduced Ian and John.

"What brings you to Stony Point?" Ian asked mildly.

"Can you possibly look at Alice and wonder that?" John asked as he turned an adoring smile toward Alice. Annie had to admit John looked dashing in his tuxedo. And Alice was lovely in the ivory strapless gown she wore. Together they made a striking couple, but a couple that Annie felt uneasy about.

Alice's gown had a full skirt with tulle crinoline under-skirts that hung nearly to the floor while the lace overskirt stopped just below the knee in front and curved to within a few inches of the tulle edge in the back. The simple color made it a perfect backdrop for the beautiful necklace of faux pearls, diamonds, and rubies that Alice wore. Long, sparkling diamond earrings caught the light each time Alice moved her head.

"You look beautiful," Annie said, giving Alice a warm hug.

"You too." Alice's smile brightened still more when she noticed Annie's hair ornament. "Oh, I'm so glad you wore something from the emerald set. I was right, it sets off your eyes."

At the word "emerald," John's interest turned sharply toward Annie's jewelry. "That is a lovely piece," he said. "Is it a family heirloom?"

"Maybe," Alice answered for her. "It came out of Annie's attic, where there are more heirlooms per square foot than an antique store."

Annie shook her head at her friend's teasing. "Only if you define 'heirloom' as 'dusty junk.' I am beginning to think none of the women in my family ever threw anything away. It all just migrated to the attic at Gram's house."

"Sounds like an excellent place for a treasure hunt," John said.

"We've had a few up there," Alice answered.

"So," Ian said, looking pointedly at John. "Do you think you'll be in Stony Point long?"

"I'm not sure," John said, locking eyes with the mayor. "It depends."

"On what?" Ian asked.

John didn't answer for a moment and the tension between the two men ramped up. Annie was struck again with how fiercely protective Ian could be. At least this time, his protective streak wasn't related to her, and she was glad of it.

Just as John seemed ready to answer the mayor's question, the ballroom was plunged into darkness. With the heavy drapes over the tall windows that lined the long, outside wall of the room, the darkness seemed absolute. Annie heard several cries of alarm and called out, "Is everyone all right?"

Then she felt a tug at her hair and wondered if Ian were trying to reach out to her in the dark. She could feel strands of hair falling down on her neck, and she suspected Ian's cuff link must have caught and pulled part of her chignon loose.

"I'm fine," Alice's voice said in the darkness.

"Are you all right, Annie?" Ian asked.

"I'm fine. Though it's amazing how wobbly it feels to be totally blind like this."

"We should stand still," John suggested. "With this crowd, we'd just bump into people if we move around."

"They probably just overloaded the circuit," Ian said calmly. "The sound equipment for the live music can draw quite a bit of power, and this is an older building."

"I can see the light from the emergency exit," Alice said and her voice sounded so close to Annie's ear that she knew her friend wasn't heeding the advice to stand still. Standing still wasn't really in Alice's nature. "So that one's on."

"That kind of light normally works even if the power goes off," Ian said. "They have batteries."

The continuing darkness made Annie feel a bit dizzy, as if she were swaying. She reached out toward the sound of Ian's voice and laid her hand on his sleeve. She instantly felt more centered and calmer.

"Well," Alice said, still standing near Annie. "Since we didn't find a mystery in the attic, one seems to have come to us here."

"I still think it'll turn out to be more electrical than mysterious," Ian answered.

"I just hope it doesn't last long," Annie said, and she felt Ian lay a reassuring hand over the one she had put on his arm.

All around the room, voices continued to call out. Annie listened quietly. Some of the people were clearly afraid, but others sounded quite insulted by the accident. She suspected the owner of Maplehurst Inn was going to get an earful from some of the guests over this.

Suddenly light flooded back into the room, and Annie let out a sigh of relief.

"Annie?"

Annie turned toward Alice with a smile.

"Where did your hair comb go?"

Annie put her hand up to her head. The hair ornament was gone! She looked around on the floor but didn't see it anywhere. Had someone grabbed it in the dark? Why would anyone go to that kind of trouble for costume jewelry?

— 9 —

"*I* felt a tug at my hair when the lights went out," Annie said. "I thought it was you, Ian."

"I didn't touch you until you put your hand on my arm," Ian said, a frown pulling at his eyebrows.

"It had to be someone close by," Alice said. "The room was dark as pitch. I can't imagine someone weaving through the crowd to get over here."

"That does make sense," Ian said, then he looked at John MacFarlane so pointedly that Annie half expected Ian to demand the other man turn out his pockets.

"It's really not worth a fuss," Annie said. "It was just costume jewelry, and it wasn't even really my style. If someone wanted it that much, I would probably have just given it to her or him." At that, Annie remembered Harry's date asking about borrowing the comb. She turned and scanned the crowd, spotting Harry and Sunny only a few couples away.

"Still," Alice said. "A jewel thief. That's a mystery for sure. Everyone at the Hook and Needle Club will love it."

"Oh, I don't want to get a whole thing started over it," Annie said. "Really."

"I still don't like the idea of someone taking something off your person," Ian said, his eyes still on John. The other man seemed intent on not noticing the mayor's interest.

"I'm glad you weren't hurt," John finally said, breaking

some of the tension from Ian's stare.

"At least it was just a hair comb," Alice said. "Imagine if it were earrings, ouch!" She reached up to rub her own ears in sympathy.

The word "earrings" made Annie think of Victoria Meyer and her odd fascination with the earrings from the set. She looked through the crowd and saw the elegant young woman was chatting with John and Gwendolyn Palmer. They were even closer to the alcove than Harry and his date. Still, that didn't make any sense at all. Why would a wealthy woman have the slightest interest in costume jewelry?

As she looked over the crowd, she saw that Jenna Paige was fairly close as well. She'd found poor Stella and was talking avidly to the older woman while Stella looked a bit desperate. Annie noticed that Simon Gunderson was nowhere to be seen. Stella's driver and general companion hovered close behind her, and Annie saw that Jason looked amused as he watched Stella and Jenna.

Just beyond Stella, Annie saw Peggy and Wally talking with Ian's brother and his wife again. As she continued to scan the crowd, she spotted a number of people she knew. Then she gave herself a little mental shake at the realization that she was compiling a suspect list. *All this mystery stuff is going to my head*, she thought.

"I believe Chief Edwards is here," Ian said. "Perhaps we should go find him and let him know about this."

"Oh, I don't really think this is a police matter," Annie said, alarmed at the thought. Since she'd come to Stony Point she'd had to bother the police plenty of times with real issues, but she always worried that Chief Edwards was eventually going to chalk her up as overly imaginative and prone to hysterics.

"You may not have been the only person to have something taken when the lights went out," Ian said. "We should ask."

Annie agreed and let Ian lead her to the chief. She nearly laughed when she saw the chief was wearing a deerstalker hat and caped coat that definitely brought Sherlock Holmes to mind. The chief greeted Ian and Annie warmly, then listened seriously to Annie's stammered explanation about the hair comb.

"I don't want to raise a fuss," Annie said. "But Ian thought you should know in case anything else went missing."

"And you're quite sure the comb isn't valuable?" the chief asked.

"I haven't had it appraised or anything like that," Annie said. "But I'm certain it was just costume jewelry."

The chief nodded. "Well, I could open a case file on it if you'd like."

"I'd rather not," Annie said, a little desperately.

"Fine," he said. "Then for now we'll just consider it an unfortunate incident, if you're OK with that. No one else has reported anything missing, yet."

Annie sighed with relief. "If no one does, I'll be happy to simply chalk it up to an unfortunate incident."

The rest of the ball passed pleasantly. Ian continued to mingle with the crowd until he'd at least greeted everyone he knew. Then they danced a bit. Finally, Annie was too tired for any more dancing, and Ian admitted he was about partied out as well. He drove her home, and Annie was again grateful to see the warm glow of Grey Gables waiting for her.

"Thank you for an interesting evening," Annie said as Ian walked her to the door.

He winced. "Ouch, that's the kiss of death. *Interesting*."

She smiled. "How about unique?"

He put a hand to his chest. "Ow, ow."

"Hmmm. Unforgettable?"

"I can live with that. I'm sorry you lost your jewelry."

"Well, being the victim of a jewel thief is definitely something *I* didn't expect. All the rich ladies would be so jealous."

Ian laughed aloud at that. "I had a wonderful time tonight, Annie Dawson. May I call on you the next time I need to look less miserable and alone?"

"Definitely." Annie gave Ian's hand a squeeze and then slipped through the front door. "Good night, Ian."

"Good night, Annie."

Annie turned away from the door, smiling softly to herself. She walked into the front room and gasped. The cushions had been pulled from the couch and thrown on the floor. Drawers stood open on the small side table. Annie backed up quickly, hurrying back to the door. "Ian!"

Ian turned. "Yes?"

"Could you come in here, please?"

At her anxious tone, Ian trotted quickly up the walk, and Annie led him into the front room. He glanced around. "Someone was looking for something. Is this the only room you've been in?"

Annie nodded, blinking back tears. She hated it whenever her home felt invaded, and that had happened far too often since returning to Stony Point. "Do you think the person might still be here?" she whispered.

"I doubt it, but let me call Chief Edwards, just in case, before we do any more exploring." He pulled out his cell phone and dialed, and then had a brief conversation with the chief. "He's on his way. He was still at the ball, but he said he was about to leave anyway."

Annie had a sudden thought that brought a slight smile. "This will be the first time my case has been examined by Sherlock Holmes."

"Good to see some of that Annie Dawson spirit."

When Chief Edwards arrived, he left the deerstalker cap in the car, but the Sherlock Holmes persona lingered as he walked through each of the downstairs rooms. Though nothing seemed to have been maliciously trashed, every drawer or cupboard door hung open and a number of objects were shifted out of place.

As they started up the stairs to check the second floor, the chief asked, "Have you noticed anything missing?"

"No," Annie said. "I can't be sure, but nothing has stood out."

When the chief opened the door to Annie's room, Boots streaked past them like a gray blur. "I'm sure I didn't leave that door closed," Annie said.

As they looked into the disheveled room, Chief Edwards said, "Since the housebreaker was clearly in this room, I expect that's who shut the cat up in the room. Look around carefully, Mrs. Dawson. Do you see anything missing?"

Annie looked around the room in alarm. Someone had opened every drawer and her clothes were in disarray within. The boxes that she'd stacked neatly in the closet until she got a chance to unpack them were now in the middle of the room, contents half spilled out. Annie stepped over to the dresser, quietly stuffing a couple of bras back in a drawer, and then she checked her jewelry box. She wasn't really into jewelry, not like Alice, but Wayne had given her an expensive watch for their last anniversary along with the diamond earrings she was wearing. The watch lay neatly in the jewelry box. The box clearly had been pawed through, but nothing taken.

"I don't understand this," Annie said. "Probably the most valuable things I own are my laptop, which is right there on the top of the dresser, and the watch that's still in the jewelry box. What could this person have wanted?"

"I don't know." The chief looked over the room quietly. "I don't suppose you have some new *mystery* you're working on?"

Annie shook her head. "Only this one tonight."

"And the hair comb," Ian added.

Annie looked startled. She'd actually forgotten the hair comb in the shock of seeing her home invaded. Losing it seemed so unimportant in the light of some stranger pawing through her underwear drawer. "But that hair comb wasn't worth much at all," she said. "The watch alone was worth more than that whole costume jewelry set."

"It's possible you're mistaken about that," the chief said. "Do you have other pieces in the set?"

Annie nodded, her eyes sweeping the room. Where had

she put that jewelry box? Then she remembered shoving it under her pillow to keep Boots out of it. She walked over to the bed where a few things from her closet had been tossed by whoever wrecked her room. The chief stepped up beside her. "Mrs. Dawson, is that blood?"

Annie looked at a several small drops of blood on the edge of one of her Battenberg lace pillowcases. "That's not mine," she said. "I'm sure I would remember injuring myself."

Ian grinned. "As I remember, Boots can get a little feisty with trespassers."

"So the housebreaker may be wearing a few scratches," the chief said. "I'll need to take the pillowcase with me. We're not exactly *CSI: New York* around here, but that blood could be evidence."

Annie nodded and shook the pillow out of the case. As she picked it up, she saw the small jewelry box underneath. "Well, they didn't take this jewelry box either," she said. She picked it up and opened it. The emerald necklace and brooch still lay in their specially molded spots. Annie ran her finger over the empty slots for the earrings and comb. "I guess the thief wasn't after these."

"Or Boots dissuaded them from messing with your bed," Ian said. "After all, not a lot of people keep jewelry boxes under their pillows. It might have seemed unlikely enough to not be worth wrestling an angry cat over."

They poked through the rest of the upstairs rooms and discovered the window in the spare bedroom was wide open and the screen shoved up. The housebreaker had clearly come in through the window after climbing up the broad oak whose branches often brushed the window on stormy nights. "I'm definitely getting someone to trim that tree back," Annie said.

The chief leaned out through the open window, judging the climb and distance. "Well, we know one thing about the housebreakers," he said. "They were young and reasonably fit."

After that, they even checked the attic where some of the closest trunks had been thrown open, but most of the boxes and trunks were clearly untouched. "I guess this was a little too daunting," Ian said. "The only way to do a thorough search up here would be to move in."

"Is anything missing here?" Chief Edwards asked.

Annie turned slowly, looking around the attic. "I'm not sure I would know. Nothing obvious."

The chief nodded. "Well, I'll file a report, and you can come in sometime tomorrow and look it over. You let me know if you find anything missing."

"I will," Annie said as they trooped down the two flights of stairs.

"I'll send one of my men to drive by the house a few times tonight," the chief said. "But I don't expect they'll be back. Someone was clearly looking for something, and they did a pretty thorough job. I see no sign that you interrupted the searchers, so I assume they simply gave up."

Annie nodded and thanked the chief. He left soon, but Ian lingered. "I hate to leave you alone after this," he said.

Annie forced a weak laugh. "Well, you'd think I'd be getting used to people poking around Grey Gables by now. Usually though, I'm at least doing some poking of my own to get it all started."

"Do you want me to stay?" Ian asked. "I could sleep on the couch."

Annie shook her head. "I'm a big girl; I can handle it."

"OK," Ian said reluctantly. As he opened the door, they were met with an excited Alice rushing up the front steps.

"I saw Chief Edwards leaving as I got home," Alice said. "Is everything all right?"

"Someone broke into Grey Gables, but other than scaring Boots half to death and making a mess, they didn't do much."

"That's enough," Alice said. "I'm putting my foot down. Either you come over and spend the night with me, or I'm staying here. You don't need to be alone after a break-in."

"I second that," Ian said.

"All right, I give," Annie said. "Would you mind staying here? I want to get at least a few things back in order. I don't think I could sleep if I didn't."

"No problem," Alice said. "Let me go get my jammies." She turned and headed back for the carriage house.

"Well, since I'm leaving you in good hands, I feel better about leaving. Thanks again for coming with me tonight. I wish the evening hadn't ended so badly."

"It was quite an evening," Annie said. "For a small town, there aren't a lot of dull moments in Stony Point."

Ian squeezed her arm gently, and then he turned and headed back to his car.

Annie walked back inside and began putting the front room in order. It was mostly a matter of arranging cushions on the couch and closing drawers. She knew her room would be a much bigger job.

Minutes later, Alice joined her. Together they made quick work of the downstairs, and then sat down for a comforting cup of chamomile tea. "I can do the rest of the cleaning tomorrow after church," Annie said.

Alice looked surprised. "I thought you might want to stay home and recover." Alice said. "Everyone would understand."

Annie took a long sip of the warm tea. "No, I'm going to do just what I would normally do. Besides, I think I would benefit from the peace of a morning at church." Then she smiled at Alice. "Let's talk about something else so I can take my mind off this before we try to sleep. So, tell me about *you*."

"You mean *me* in relation to John?" Alice said. "I still don't know what he wants, but I'm sure he wasn't lured here by any undying love for me."

"I could see someone lured by exactly that," Annie said. "But I agree that this isn't likely to be the case here. Has he said anything to give you an idea of what his real motives are?"

"He has asked me how my businesses are going," Alice said, and then she sighed. "Honestly, I expect it's money somehow. John was always overspending and getting involved in one sure-fire deal or another. It took me *forever* to get my credit in decent shape after the divorce. If Betsy hadn't vouched for me, I never could have gotten the landlord to rent me the carriage house."

"Well, at least you know to be careful," she said.

"Oh, I'm careful. I checked to make sure I didn't

have any rings missing after he held my hand," she said. "He practically drooled over the diamonds on that Meyer woman."

Annie smiled a little at her practical friend checking her jewelry, and then she blinked as a wave of exhaustion passed over her. "I think I'm done in."

Alice took the guest room and Annie spent the night surrounded by the familiarity of Gram's bedroom, which had now become her own. Sometime in the night, she felt a light thump and heard Boots purr as she curled up against Annie's back. With the comforting warmth and gentle rumble of the purr, Annie fell back to sleep.

～ 10 ～

The next morning, Alice helped Annie put the upstairs back in order before she left to do a little light cleaning at her own place. Although the house no longer showed signs of the break-in, Annie still felt restless. Several times, she opened the jewelry box and stared at the remaining pieces of the emerald jewelry set. They were pretty, but she couldn't really say they looked real. She wondered if she should get an appraiser to look at them. At least knowing the actual value of the pieces would help her nail down one aspect of this mystery.

Finally, she shoved the box in her needlecraft bag and finished getting ready for church. *I need some time to think about something besides the break-in*, she thought as she headed out to her car. Still, it was hard to set aside the nagging thought that, whether it made sense or not, somehow the costume jewelry had something to do with all that had happened.

The morning service soothed Annie's troubled nerves, and she carried that bit of peace home with her. On Monday she spent the day close to home and again fought the urge to peer out the window for burglars. She needed to do something to get rid of that terrible feeling of violation. She hoped her friends would have some ideas on Tuesday when they met for the Hook and Needle Club.

The next day, the warm smiles of the other women sitting in the cozy chairs at A Stitch in Time made Annie feel better instantly, giving her almost as much of a rush of security and peace as the church visit had. Stony Point might be a little too mysterious sometimes, but it was full of good friends.

"I had such a wonderful time at the ball!" Peggy gushed as soon as Annie sat down. "I'll bring back the gown and jewelry as soon as I get the dress cleaned."

Annie smiled at her. "You may keep the gown as far as I'm concerned. It's just one more thing in the attic. And I can't imagine it looking nearly as good on anyone else as it did on you."

"That's for sure," Alice said. "You looked like a 1940s movie star."

Peggy blushed slightly at the compliments. "Wally did say he liked the dress," she admitted. "I don't know where I would wear it again, but you never know!"

The mention of Wally reminded Annie, "Peggy, would Wally know anyone who trims trees? I need the oak trimmed away from the upstairs windows."

"Because of the break-in?" Kate asked sympathetically, laying the vest she was crocheting in her lap as she looked at Annie.

Annie glanced around in surprise, and then she turned her eyes to Alice. Her friend held up her hands. "Don't blame me. Ian must have talked to Chief Edwards in front of Charlotte because everyone already knew when I got here."

Peggy blushed again, looking down very pointedly at the quilt square in her lap. "Charlotte was in the diner this morning for breakfast. She told me about the gang that climbed your tree to rob your house."

"Well, I don't know that it was a gang or even more than one person," Annie said, smiling slightly. "And it still doesn't look like anyone took anything. But the tree climbing is right."

"Why would anyone break into your house?" Stella asked, so surprised that she actually stopped knitting—something that rarely happened when Stella was at their meetings.

"I guess they thought Annie had something they wanted," Alice said, looking pointedly at Stella.

When Annie had first come to Stony Point, Stella had hired someone to buy something from Annie in secret. The man took his assignment a bit too seriously and tried to break into Grey Gables. Stella must have thought of that when Alice made her remark, as a small dot of color appeared on the elderly woman's pale cheeks, and her knitting needles began clicking furiously. "Do you have any idea what it might be?" Stella asked quietly.

"I'm not sure," Annie said. "I do have an idea, but it seems so silly." She went on to explain about the comb that had been snatched from her hair when the lights went out at the ball. And she described that rather unusual place she'd left the rest of the set and the signs of Boots's response to the housebreaker.

"Good for Boots!" Mary Beth said. "I'll have to buy that kitty a new mouse."

"Maybe I'll save her some fish scraps from the diner," Peggy said. "A hero like that deserves a reward."

Annie laughed. "Well, Boots is always up for more food."

"You know, this gives us one more clue to the culprit," Alice said. "It sounds like whoever broke into the house is going to have some scratches."

"So our first step is to check hands," Peggy said. "Everyone comes into The Cup & Saucer at one time or another. I'll watch for suspicious scratches. Though it would help if we could come up with some suspects."

"Who was standing near you when the lights went out?" Gwen asked, dropping her own knitting project into her lap as she turned her full interest to the new mystery. "I know that ballroom was pitch dark. I can't imagine anyone walking very far to reach you."

"Well, Ian was beside me," Annie said. "In fact, I thought at first the tug on my hair was him, reaching out to make sure I was OK. And Alice was there with John MacFarlane."

Alice narrowed her eyes. "John did look awfully interested in that comb."

"But if you didn't get home until after I did, he couldn't have been the person who broke into my house," Annie said. "Besides, I mentioned that it was costume jewelry after it disappeared, so John would have no reason to break into my house. By then, he knew it wasn't valuable even if he had grabbed the comb."

"You have a good point. I'd forgotten you said something about the comb being costume jewelry. Still, he could have gotten to your house," Alice said. "Not long after you went looking for Chief Edwards with Ian, John managed to spill wine on his suit, and he went off to the bathroom to dab it off. I didn't see him again for quite a while, and when he finally rejoined me, he scolded *me* like I was hard to find. Plus, we don't actually know, for sure, that the hair comb and the break-in are connected. I'm still going to do some sleuthing about the hair comb. I wouldn't put anything past John."

"He does seem a likely suspect if the only people near you were Ian, Alice, and John," Mary Beth said sensibly. "How far could someone travel in a crowded room in the pitch dark?"

"Although John might have been closest, there were plenty of other people who could have reached me in very few steps," Annie said, then she turned toward Gwen. "We were standing in that little alcove near where you were chatting with Victoria Meyer. After the comb was gone, I noticed Jenna Paige was really quite close as well. And I practically could have reached out and touched Harry and Sunny." Suddenly Annie realized what she'd said and fell silent, turning sharply to look at Kate. The last time Kate thought someone else was interested in Harry, the result had been unpleasant—especially since Annie was the some-one else Kate had suspected!

Kate looked distressed, but she forced a smile. "I know Harry was out with another woman," she said. "I had to expect it eventually. He's a good-looking man, and we are divorced. Anyway, you know Vanessa couldn't keep silent about *that*." Then Kate dropped her voice slightly and add-ed. "I know it's tacky of me to even ask, but did the woman really look like a streetwalker?"

Alice gave a tiny bark of surprised laughter at that.

"She was dressed a little ... obviously," Annie said. "But

I think Vanessa might have been letting her anger color her description."

Kate nodded. "I thought that might be the case."

Annie pursed her lips thoughtfully for a moment, and then said, "I hate to even suggest this, but that young woman Harry was with did ask if she could borrow the hair comb. I thought that was a little bold for a perfect stranger."

"Vanessa would be delighted if she turned out to be a jewel thief," Kate said. "She kept an eagle eye on them all evening and said they left early. In fact, she said, 'Dad must have had to get her home before her curfew.'"

Again Alice laughed. "She wasn't *that* young."

"Honestly, I don't know which of us is going to have more trouble adjusting to Harry dating—Vanessa or me."

"So we have two suspects!" Gwen said, pulling everyone's attention back to the mystery. "This is very exciting."

"Three," Stella added. "Annie said that young biologist was close by as well. I don't trust that young woman. She is entirely too nosy about Stony Point business. And visiting biologists would be an excellent cover for a pair of professional jewel thieves."

Annie smiled slightly. "You'd think professional jewel thieves could tell costume jewelry from real. There were many women in that room with jewelry worth a great deal more than that hair comb."

Stella sniffed. "I still think she's a viable suspect."

"What if we break up in teams and track down clues?" Peggy asked excitedly. "We could each pick our favorite suspect. I think Alice's ex is the prime suspect. Plus, he's a terrible tipper." When everyone turned to look at her, she shrugged sheepishly. "I'm just adding information."

"So we're a team," Alice said to Peggy. "I may have a plan for a bit of sleuthing."

"Oh, do be careful," Annie said. "I don't want to be the cause of any trouble."

Gwen reached out and patted Annie on the hand. "Don't worry, we're going to get to the bottom of this. I have to agree with Stella that those scientists are very suspicious," Gwen said. "I don't mean to be unkind, but you have to admit that all those questions are not normal behavior for two researchers whose minds should be on lobsters."

"I suppose I could get Jason to make some inquiries about the two of them," Stella said. "I really would prefer not to interact with that young woman more than I have to. She was entirely too familiar at that ball."

Annie couldn't imagine what Jason would think of being dragged into her sleuthing. She was surprised to hear that Stella wanted to take part at all. Stella usually considered Annie's mysteries a bit silly.

"I can't ask questions about Harry's girlfriend," Kate said quietly. "It just wouldn't look good. Though, honestly, part of me wouldn't mind her being a suspect."

Mary Beth patted her assistant on the arm. "No problem," she said. "I'll take point on that investigation. Though it would help if we knew more about her so I knew where to start."

"Well," Kate said, "Vanessa did drill her father for information, so I might be able to give you some ideas of where to start. But then I have to stay out of it."

"We seem to have cut Annie out of her own mystery,"

Peggy said. "Who do you want to investigate?"

"I think I'll investigate the jewelry," Annie said. "Maybe if we knew more about them, we'd know who might be interested in them."

"What's your plan?" Alice asked.

"I'm thinking I might get them appraised," she said. "Does anyone know who to see?"

"I have used a jeweler in Storm Harbor," Stella said, rummaging in her bag and pulling out a pen and small pad of paper. "I can give you the name and directions to get there."

"If there's a single real stone in any of those pieces," Alice said, "I'll eat my Princessa Jewelry catalog."

"I'm terribly curious about this jewelry," Mary Beth said. "What does it look like?"

"Actually, I have it here," Annie pulled out the small jewelry box from her needlepoint bag. She opened the box to show off the remaining pieces.

"It's certainly pretty," Gwen said as Annie passed the jewelry box around. "But I agree with Alice; this is definitely costume jewelry."

When the box reached Stella, the old woman stared at the jewelry with her brows furrowed. "These pieces look familiar somehow," she said finally. "I don't know where, but I'm almost certain I've seen them before."

"Maybe you saw them on Betsy?" Mary Beth suggested.

"Oh no," Stella said with a slight smile. "These aren't Betsy's style at all. Betsy always preferred the simple and the classic."

"That's what I thought," Annie said. "But it's interesting

that they look familiar to you. Could Gram have showed them to you?"

"I don't think so." The elderly woman lifted the necklace gently from the box and let it dangle from her hand. "I think I've seen them *on* someone." She laid the necklace back in the box and handed it to Annie. "I'll let you know if it comes to me."

The meeting began to break up soon after that, though each mystery-hunting team whispered plans for seeking out clues. Annie looked ruefully at her project bag; she hadn't even pulled her sweater out of the bag.

As Annie headed out to the street, she blinked a bit as a boisterous autumn breeze tossed a lock of hair into her face. Absently, she tucked it behind her ear and decided to grab a cup of coffee and a snack at The Cup & Saucer and plan her trip to Storm Harbor on Wednesday. She wanted to be certain she had thought through questions to ask the jeweler, though most of the questions that filled her head wouldn't be answered by an appraisal.

Why did the jewelry look familiar to Stella? Annie knew Stella had spent many years away from Stony Point, living in New York City. So, if she dimly remembered the jewelry, that suggested they must have belonged to an older person in either Stony Point or New York. *But it certainly wasn't an old lady who climbed my oak tree*, Annie thought.

"You look deep in thought."

Annie turned sharply to see Ian stepping up on the sidewalk. She'd not noticed him crossing the street. "Pondering my new mystery," she said.

"Speaking of which," he said, "did you sleep all right

after I left Saturday night? I saw you in church on Sunday, but you left so quickly."

"I'm sleeping OK. Of course, I've been spending the nights with a guard cat beside me."

"Boots is formidable," Ian agreed. "But I'll feel better when we know who broke into your house."

"I have found myself watching out the windows more than usual," Annie admitted with a sigh. "Do you think Chief Edwards will figure it out?"

"I'd never underestimate him."

Suddenly a thought struck Annie, and she groaned. "With all the talk about the mystery, I never got an answer from Peggy about whether Wally knew a tree trimmer. I really hoped to get the oak cut back right away. I think I'll feel safer when I know there can't possibly be a repeat of the Saturday night break-in."

"We locked the window, so it will be harder to get in," Ian said. "But you *do* need that tree trimmed. When I get back to my office, I'll call and send someone over to do it."

"Oh, I didn't mean for you to have to do it. I can call if you'll give me the name."

"I'd *like* to do it. So, are you heading to the diner? Maybe we could share a table. I haven't had lunch yet."

"That would be nice," Annie said.

Peggy actually followed them in as she'd practically run from the needlework shop to the diner, a bit late as usual after a Hook and Needle Club meeting. "Can I get you both a table?" she asked.

"Wow, it's not every day that my waitress runs to serve me," Ian answered.

"I can't let someone else steal two of my favorite customers," Peggy answered, grinning as she led them to a table near the window. Ian ordered a Reuben sandwich and soup, and Annie asked for a light salad.

"Got it," Peggy said. "Just let me clock in, and I'll bring your coffee." She turned and wove her way back to the kitchen.

Ian folded his hands on the table and smiled. "So, are the ladies of the Hook and Needle Club on the case yet?"

"Funny you should mention that," Annie said. She explained how they had already known about the mystery when she got to the meeting.

"Sorry about that," Ian said. "I think Charlotte missed her calling when she became an office manager. Clearly she was meant to be a reporter. I'll speak to her."

Annie raised her hands in mock surrender. "Not on my behalf, I hope. She scares me enough as it is. I can't imagine what she'd be like if she were actually mad at me."

"I'll keep you out of it."

Peggy appeared with a coffeepot to fill the mugs on the table, and then she leaned over and whispered almost loud enough to be heard around the room. "Alice and I are working on a plan," she said. "It's going to be just like a movie!"

"Just make sure you don't do anything crazy."

Peggy just winked at her and hurried on to the next table.

"A plan?" Ian asked.

"The club divvied up the suspects," Annie said. "I'm not sure if they think we're in an Agatha Christie novel or an episode of *Scooby Doo*."

Ian laughed. "So who are your suspects?"

Annie told him what had gone on at the meeting and why each team chose their suspect.

"Well, my vote would go to John MacFarlane," Ian said. "And I wouldn't mind having an excuse to encourage him to finish his business and leave Stony Point."

"Oh?"

Ian sighed. "You know, I knew Alice when we were teenagers. She's a few years younger than me, but everyone knew and liked Alice. Her adventures were legendary. She always had a plan, and she always seemed to be able to get a half dozen of the kids from school to go along with it." He paused and chuckled in remembrance.

"Yeah, she was like that when I used to spend summers with my grandparents," Annie said.

He nodded. "But she wasn't like that at all when she came back to Stony Point after her divorce. If Betsy hadn't dragged her out of the carriage house now and then, no one would have ever seen her. It's only since you came back to Stony Point that Alice has begun to be Alice again. I don't want to see John MacFarlane change that."

Annie nodded, not knowing what else to say. She didn't want to see that either.

~ 11 ~

With the bulk of the summer tourists gone, the drive to Storm Harbor on Wednesday was unexpectedly pleasant. Anne's thoughts rolled over and over through her list of suspects. None of it really made sense, and the mental exercise left Annie feeling uncomfortable, as if she were missing something that she ought to see.

Stella had written excellent directions, and Annie soon pulled up in front of Koenig's Jewelry, a small store squished between two others in the cramped style that Annie had begun to think of as "New England-tight" architecture.

Inside, a young man with friendly brown eyes and an prominently large nose greeted her. "Welcome to Koenig's. May I help you?"

"I'm looking for Milton Koenig," Annie said.

"That would be me," the young man said. "Or my dad or my grandfather. But since I'm the only Milt Koenig here at the moment, I claim the title. How can I help you?"

"I was hoping to get some costume jewelry appraised." Annie pulled the flat wooden box from her project bag. "Stella Brickson recommended I come here."

"Ah, Mrs. Brickson has been a valued customer of Koenig's for many, many years." Milt suddenly broke into a sheepish grin. "Maybe you shouldn't tell her I added that second 'many.'"

"Your secret is safe with me," Annie said. She placed the

jewelry box on the counter. "So, do you think you can tell me about these?"

Milt Koenig opened the box and Annie saw a faint ghost of surprise pass over his face. He gently picked up the necklace and then the brooch, looking at each gem with a jeweler's glass. "You do know this is costume jewelry?" he said. "None of these gems are real."

"I thought that was the case."

"Are you interested in selling these pieces?" Milt said. "I'd be interested in buying if you are."

"I'm mostly looking for information," Annie said. "But I'm curious—why would you be interested in a partial set of costume jewelry?"

"Sentiment, mostly," he said. "My grandfather made these, and he's gone now, so I wouldn't mind owning them for sentimental reasons."

Annie felt a wash of excitement. "How do you know your grandfather made them? Have you seen them before?"

Milt Koenig shook his head. "No, not these pieces. But my grandfather designed a lot of jewelry for wealthy families around here. It became quite the 'thing' for a while for women to own Koenig originals." He tapped the necklace. "My grandfather often used nature to inspire his designs, especially trees. But it was always a bit abstract and always asymmetrical in really subtle ways. On first glance, you just see the glitz, but then when you live with the piece a while, you can see the tree, or vine, or flower."

"Is there any way I could find out who commissioned this set?" Annie asked. "Does your family keep records?"

"My grandfather kept a portfolio of photographs of every piece he ever designed," Milt said. "He would sit in his battered old wing chair every evening and leaf through the pages. He said every piece told him a story, and remembering their stories always inspired him to create new ones. You wouldn't believe how many times my dad found the old man asleep in his chair with the book in his lap."

"Do you have that portfolio?" Annie asked.

Milt shook his head sadly. "My grandfather had another habit as he sat in that chair. He smoked. And one night, I guess he fell sleep with a cigarette burning. I was away in college at the time, and my folks were out for the evening to some fund-raiser. My grandfather died in the fire, and that portfolio went with him."

"Oh, I'm so sorry," Annie said.

"Thank you." Then Milt seemed to think of something. "I know my dad has a kind of scrapbook of his own too. It's almost all photos from newspapers and such—pictures of rich folks in Pop's jewelry. It's kind of a long shot, but this set could be in that. I don't remember seeing it, but it's not impossible. The photos are grainy and old; I don't spend a lot of time looking at them."

"Oh, could you check? And let me know if you find it?"

"Sure," Milt said. "The scrapbook's not in the store, but I can check it out for you and give you a call. You didn't say, would you consider selling me the jewelry?"

"I'd like to find out a little more about it first," Annie said. "But I promise not to sell it to anyone else without discussing it with you first. How's that?"

"I'll take it," Milt said. "Hey, would you mind if I took a snapshot of these pieces? That way I can compare them against the scrapbook and maybe show them to my dad. He might have seen them before."

"That would be very nice."

Annie was excited to have gotten even an inch closer to solving the mystery of who owned the jewelry. Somehow, she felt the break-in was tied to the jewelry whether it made sense or not. Once she knew who had owned the jewels, she knew some of the other pieces would fall into place.

Milt quickly snapped his photos and took Annie's name and phone number. "I'll let you know whatever I find out," he promised.

When Annie left the little shop, she paused on the street a moment, taking deep breaths of the cool fall air. Storm Harbor wasn't quite as neat or charming as Stony Point. The style of the buildings was similar, but they looked more worn and tired.

Across the street and up a few storefronts, she saw a small restaurant and tavern. She had no interest in the tavern part, but considered grabbing a cup of coffee or a nice bowl of chowder before heading back to Stony Point. Something warming sounded really good, and the small salad she'd had for lunch didn't seem to be sticking with her.

She strode across the street and slipped inside the dark restaurant. As her eyes adjusted to the gloom, Annie wondered if she'd made a poor choice. She never really liked eating in dark places and tended to wonder if the shadows could be hiding poor hygiene. But before she could turn around, a lanky young man in a white shirt and low-hanging black pants asked her to follow him.

He led Annie to a tiny booth in an especially dark spot

where a candle flickered. Annie wondered if it would give enough light to read a menu.

"Your server will be Sunny."

Annie looked up, startled, but the man had already turned and was headed briskly back to the front podium. She had certainly not come here looking for Harry's new girlfriend, but Sunny wasn't an extremely common name.

As she expected, she recognized the blonde right away as she headed for the table. Sunny wore the black and white that seemed to be the waitstaff uniform, though Sunny had added a silky white scarf tied around her neck that helped only slightly in obscuring the fact that half the buttons on the waitress's tight shirt were unbuttoned. "Didn't I just see you at that fancy party?" Sunny asked. "You were babysitting Harry's kid or something, right?"

"Vanessa doesn't need a sitter," Annie said mildly. "She's a teenager."

"If she's like I was as a teenager, she needs more than a babysitter." Sunny snorted laughter. "What can I get you?"

Annie opened the menu and tried to read the print by the candlelight. Eventually, she gave up. "What kind of soups do you have?"

"Tomato, chicken noodle, clam chowder," Sunny said as she ticked them off on her fingers. "Chili and beef with vegetable." Then she leaned over the table, displaying a disquieting amount of cleavage. "They're all out of a can though. You could get them cheaper at the grocery."

"Maybe just a hot cup of coffee," Annie said finally.

"Coming right up!" When Sunny reached out for the menu, Annie looked over her hands and forearms. She saw no sign of scratches. But who knows what might lie under that scarf?

"Oh, and Sunny?" Annie added before the waitress could dash away. "Do you know if they ever found out why the lights went out at the party?"

"I dunno," Sunny said. "But Harry bashed his knee on a table in the dark." Sunny giggled. "It's a good thing his kid wasn't around right then. Harry's got quite a mouth on him, and I'm sure that uptight ex of his wouldn't want the kid learning any new vocabulary. Anyway, when the lights came on, Harry said old places like that sometimes have wiring problems."

"So, are you and Harry dating regularly?"

"Dating," She giggled again. "That's so old-fashioned. No, Harry and I don't *date* much, though he stays over at my place sometimes when he's had a little too much fun here, if you get what I mean. Harry told me his parents were going to that shindig, and they wanted him to come. Honestly, I think he just didn't know who else to ask. His folks aren't real friendly people though, so I don't know why Harry bothered. He says they're on his case a lot."

"Did anyone take anything from you when the lights went out?" Annie asked, not wanting to get into gossip about Harry and his family.

"No, though I think Harry was trying to grab something when he slammed into the table." She giggled again. "I told him that's what he gets for being a perv. I better go get your coffee. My boss can be a real jerk about my chatting up the customers."

Sunny brought her coffee promptly but didn't stay to

talk. The coffee was hot but had a bitter burnt flavor, and Annie found herself missing The Cup & Saucer terribly. When Sunny brought her bill, Annie held it close to the candle to read the server name scrawled on the bottom—Sunny Day.

"Is Sunny Day a stage name or something?" Annie asked.

"Nope," Sunny said. "My mom just really liked Sesame Street."

Annie blinked at her in confusion.

"You know, the Sesame Street song?" the young woman said as she began to sing. "Sunny day, chasin' the clouds away."

"Oh, that's really nice."

"I like it," Sunny said as she took the money Annie handed her. "I'll be right back with your change."

"No, you just keep the rest," Annie said as she stood up to go.

"Oh, that's sweet. I hope you'll come back. I could use more customers like you."

Annie smiled vaguely, though inwardly she vowed never to come back to the dark little place again. She gathered her purse and headed for the door. Just before she reached it, Sunny called out to her. Annie waited for the young woman to catch up with her.

"That inn was real ritzy," Sunny said. "Do you know if they might be hiring?" She leaned a little closer to Annie. "This place is kind of a dump. With a ritzy clientele, a girl might get ahead, you know?"

"I really don't know if they're hiring," Annie said.

Sunny frowned, but nodded. "Thanks anyway. I don't

suppose you know the owners? Maybe you could put in a good word?"

"I would," Annie said. "But I am fairly new to Stony Point, and I don't actually know the owners of Maplehurst Inn."

"Oh." Sunny drooped a bit, but then forced a smile. "Well, thanks for the nice tip anyway."

"You're welcome."

Annie felt an instant lift in her mood when she left the shadowy restaurant and emerged on the street where the low afternoon sun bathed everything in a warm yellow glow.

Annie wasn't completely sure what she'd learned in Storm Harbor, but she suspected she was collecting puzzle pieces. They might seem oddly shaped right now, and she didn't know where they fit, but she still felt like she was moving ahead.

When she finally reached Grey Gables, long shadows were beginning to stretch across the lawn. Annie was surprised to see a small cherry-picker machine already parked in her spot on the drive. The long arm of the machine reached into the oak where a man cut branches with a small chain saw, while another collected them after they fell and fed them to a wood chipper.

Annie drove a bit farther and parked in Alice's drive, and then walked back across the lawn to her own house. As she approached, the man in the tree shut off his chain saw and the other turned and waved. "Mayor Butler sent us over," he said, tipping back his hard hat. "He said this was a rush job."

"I'm certainly going to sleep easier knowing it's done,"

she admitted. They talked only a few minutes more, mostly about how much the job would cost, and then Annie left them to their work.

When she went in the house, she was a little surprised not to be met by Boots. The gray cat normally could be counted on to spend a while scolding Annie for leaving her alone to starve. "Boots, here kitty, kitty," she called but no answering padding footsteps sounded. "What now?"

Annie walked nervously through the downstairs, looking for the cat. She was relieved to see that nothing seemed out of place, but she also didn't find the cat in any of her normal napping spots. Finally, Annie climbed the stairs.

She checked her bedroom, expecting to find Boots on the bed, but although she did see a cat-shaped imprint on her quilt, she didn't find the cat. She walked down the hall to the guest room, even though Boots never went in there.

She heard Boots growling before she saw her. The gray cat was standing on the wide windowsill, glaring out at the man in the cherry picker. The cat's tail lashed the air, and she hissed.

"Oh Boots!" Annie said. "Those are actually the good guys."

The cat turned and looked at her. Annie scooped Boots up and scratched the cat under the chin as she carried her out of the spare room. "Did that big machine scare you?" she cooed.

She carried Boots to the kitchen and filled her dinner bowl, which went a long way toward soothing the cat's unsettled nerves. The tree trimmers soon finished their job, and Annie thanked them gratefully, tacking a nice tip onto the price of the trimming. She'd feel much safer knowing she didn't have a ladder growing right next to her upstairs window.

Night falls fast on the New England coast, and Annie walked through the house, carefully checking all the locks on the windows and doors. She hated feeling nervous in her own home. She tried to get caught up in a novel and then television, but she finally had to admit to herself that she couldn't concentrate so she settled on the front-room sofa with her crocheting.

The movement of the hook and feel of the soft, warm yarn through her fingers was soothing. When Annie was a little girl, Gram had noticed her tendency to be restless. "It always helps to have something to do with your hands," Gram had said. "If you keep your hands busy, you can pour that nervous energy right out through your fingers."

As usual, Gram had been right. Though Annie couldn't lose herself in cross-stitch the way Betsy Holden did, she had found her crafting niche in the warmth of crochet. *Hooking the yarn, coaxing it through the loops of the pattern is a lot like solving a mystery,* Annie thought. *You have to hit the right loops to make the pattern work out. If you don't it'll just be a scrambled mess of yarn.*

"So where are the right loops in this mystery?" she said aloud.

Boots glanced at her from the other corner of the sofa, but didn't offer any kitty insights.

Annie jumped, knocking a ball of yarn to the floor when the doorbell rang. She quickly chased the rolling ball, but Boots got to it first, and Annie had to pry the kitty claws out of it and stuff the whole project back in her bag.

The doorbell rang again as Annie finally walked to the entry. She flipped on the porch light and saw Alice standing on the porch. Relieved to see her friend, she pulled open the door.

"I'm glad you're all right," Alice said as Annie stepped back to let her in. "I saw your car in my drive and wondered if you'd had another break-in."

"Oh, I'm sorry. I forgot I had parked over there. Ian sent some men to trim that oak tree, and their machinery took up my whole drive."

"Wow, that's fast. Our mayor really knows how to get things done ...," Alice said, adding with a mischievous gleam, "... when he has the right motivation."

Annie shook her head at her friend. "He was just worried, and I have to admit that I feel better now."

"Well enough to hear about my sleuthing mission?" Alice asked.

"Of course," Annie said. "Let me put on the kettle."

They were soon settled in the kitchen, and Alice told Annie about her afternoon. Alice had spent the afternoon hanging out around Maplehurst Inn, waiting for Peggy to call her as soon as John MacFarlane showed up at The Cup & Saucer for supper.

"How did you know he wouldn't just eat at the inn?" Annie asked.

"The diner is cheaper," Alice said. "With no one to impress, John usually has to go with cheaper."

Annie nodded, and Alice went on to tell her she'd gotten the call and headed up to John's room.

"How on earth did you get in his room?" Annie asked.

"Well, let's just say that someone on the cleaning staff is a Divine Décor customer," Alice said. "And maybe another has an ex who gives her trouble too."

"Oh, that's devious," Annie said, "and I don't think Chief Edwards would approve."

"Do you want to hear this report?"

"OK, OK." Annie raised her hands in surrender.

"So I searched his room, and I didn't find the hair comb," Alice said. "I couldn't see how he could hock it that fast. The room has a safe, but he hadn't even locked it, and all it had in it was a pair of slippers."

"Slippers?"

Alice shrugged. "Anyway, I had my arm under the mattress, rooting around when John came back."

"Oh no."

"Oh yes," Alice said. "Apparently I accidentally shut off my cell phone after I'd gotten the call from Peggy, and I missed her panicked call letting me know he was coming back."

"What happened?"

"It was a little sticky at first, but I just went on the offensive. I told him I wasn't buying any kind of love and romance reason for him to be in Stony Point, and I wanted him to come clean. He admitted he was actually back here to see what kind of financial shape I was in. The rat tried to hit me up for money!"

"He certainly has nerve," Annie said.

"He always had plenty of that. Anyway, he swore he didn't have anything to do with your hair comb. He said if he was going to try being a jewel thief there were a lot more appealing targets. He had a point. Some of those women were dripping with real jewels."

"So you believe him?"

"I think I do," Alice said. "I mean, John is a rat. And I would definitely count my silver and check my jewelry box if I let him come visit *me*, but grabbing a comb out of your hair really doesn't seem like him. He'd rob you, but he'd be smooth about it."

Then she smiled slightly. "I also checked his face, neck, and hands: no scratch marks. He definitely wasn't the housebreaker that Boots tangled with."

"So that doesn't really get us any closer to solving the case," Annie said.

"Sorry. I guess it doesn't."

"What are you going to do about John?"

"After the things I said in his room, I'm not sure I'm going to have to do anything. I'd be surprised if he hung around. He told me he'd noticed he wasn't very popular in town, so that should keep him from begging money from anyone else."

"I guess eliminating someone is progress," Annie said. "Even if I don't really feel any closer to an answer."

~ 12 ~

Annie headed to bed soon after Alice left. When Annie moved to Stony Point, she initially had slept in her old room from summers with her grandparents. But after a while, she was naturally drawn to Gram's bedroom. Not only did it have a spectacular view of the ocean, but something about staying in that room made her feel a little less alone. And she was sure it wasn't just the way Boots slept all over her. She simply felt wrapped in good memories when she curled up in Gram's bed.

The next day, Annie headed outside for some leaf raking as soon as the dew dried. She hoped it would work like crocheting and soothe her jumpy nerves. She was pleased to see that the men who'd cut limbs from the oak had swept up most of the leaves when they cleaned the debris from the tree trimming.

"One leaf pile down," Annie said. "A dozen to go." She turned to rake leaves away from the house and saw footprints in the soft soil near the house. She figured it was just the shoe prints of the tree trimmers and raked the ground a bit to smooth them over. As she continued around the house, pulling leaves away from the foundation, she found more and more prints. Why would the tree trimmers have circled the house? There was only one oak in the yard, so they couldn't have been confused about which tree to cut.

She looked carefully at each print she found. She was no expert, but they looked alike to her. Were they prints left from the break-in? Or had someone come last night to prowl around the house?

"It couldn't have been last night," she told herself reasonably. "They wouldn't have been covered with leaves." But she didn't quite buy that argument. With the blustery fall winds, the leaves shifted places constantly and collected quickly close to the house. A chill crept up Annie's spine, and she struggled to shrug it off. She fished her cell phone out of her pocket and used it to take photos of all the tracks she could find. She even went back in the house and found a ruler so she could take a photo of one print with the ruler beside it to show its length.

Annie held her own foot next to the print. Her own shoe was considerably smaller. That might mean the person was a man. Of course, she'd noticed the teenaged girls in the craft club also had bigger feet than her. If each generation kept getting bigger feet, eventually they'd all wear clown shoes. So, bigger feet didn't automatically mean a man.

She squatted down and looked closely at the muddy imprint. It was the perfect shape of a foot with a distinct heel but no real tread pattern at all. It was almost as if the bottom of the shoe was smooth. Men's dress shoes?

Finally, she accepted she was no expert. She walked to the carriage house, picked up her car from Alice's drive and headed into town. She'd show Chief Edwards the photos and let him decide if he wanted to send anyone out. Annie soon pulled up in front of Town Hall and went in search of the chief. He looked over her cell phone photos seriously.

"That was real good thinking with the ruler," he said.

Annie thanked him, but she wasn't sure if the chief might be patronizing her a bit. He didn't jump up and offer to send anyone out to take casts of the prints, though he did have her e-mail the photos from her phone to his computer. Annie was more than a little embarrassed when he had to show her how to do it.

"I'm afraid I mostly use my phone as a phone," she said.

The chief chuckled. "Pretty soon they'll invent a cell phone that does everything but live your life for you," he said.

Annie was feeling a little let down as she left Town Hall. She wasn't certain what she'd been expecting. She just felt stalled on the mystery and a little frustrated.

"Annie! Annie!"

Annie looked up at the shout and spotted Gwen Palmer in front of the Stony Point Savings Bank on the other side of the Town Square. Annie waved back, but Gwen hurried across the street and started walking across the Town Square grass.

It must be important, Annie thought as she saw Gwen struggle with her high heels in the soft ground. "You wait there," Annie called. "I'll come to you." Annie's soft-soled, slip-on oxfords were much better suited for the grassy square.

She soon crossed the distance and met Gwen on the sidewalk where the older woman had retreated to wipe mud from her shoes.

"Oh Annie, I wanted to tell you what I learned," Gwen said. "I was in the bank this morning, and I saw that biologist opening a bank account. The man."

Annie smiled. "I'm not sure that's totally mysterious."

"Why open an account if you're only going to be here for a couple weeks?" Gwen said, raising her eyebrows. "And I noticed something else. That young man had a bandage on his hand. Maybe he's covering up cat scratches."

Annie had to admit that was interesting, but hardly conclusive. "They've been out on fishing boats," she said reasonably. "I imagine it's fairly easy to get small injuries in their work."

"I know," Gwen said. "That's why Stella is going to suffer for the cause and chat up Jenna Paige. Apparently that girl thinks Stella wants to be her new best friend. Stella has been practically hiding at home to avoid her. But she promised to be at A Stitch in Time this afternoon. That's when Mary Beth told us Jenna is coming in to get some help with her cross-stitch."

"Stella doesn't do cross-stitch," Annie said.

"No, but you know if she's there, she'll be able to chat with the girl."

That did *seem* likely. "You know Jenna Paige may be a perfectly nice girl," Annie said. "She's just a bit eager."

Gwen sniffed, and for a moment Annie was struck with how much she sounded like Stella. "I'm not saying she's definitely the perp," Gwen said, using the term she had heard from a TV crime show. "We're not going to accuse her of anything. Stella's just going to grill her."

Annie had to struggle not to laugh at the thought of the austere Stella grilling anyone, but she said she was looking forward to hearing the results of that.

"That's good," Gwen said, "because we're going to call an emergency meeting of the Hook and Needle Club tomorrow so everyone can compare notes. I want to hear how the others are doing on the case too."

"OK," Annie said, again struggling not to smile at how much Gwen had embraced detective vocabulary. "I'll be there."

Annie drove home, deep in thought. She was greeted by Boots, begging for food as usual. The demanding meows were so familiar that Annie found the sound comforting. She scooped Boots up and carried her to the kitchen. "I'm glad I can always count on you," she said as Boots rubbed her head against Annie's chin, "or count on your stomach anyway."

Annie poured a small bit of food in the small ceramic dish with cute fishes painted on it. Boots glanced into the bowl and then back up at Annie. "You already had some guilt kibble this morning before I left," Annie reminded her. Boots didn't look convinced, but she started gobbling the food just the same.

As Annie patted the chubby cat, her own stomach growled, and she decided on a quick sandwich and cup of soup. She sat next to the kitchen window and stared out at the leafy lawn. Now and then, an eddy of wind would pick up a leaf and spin it around.

After cleaning up, Annie tried to settle down on the couch to work on her sweater project, but she quickly remembered that she'd meant to have Kate help her with the mess she'd made of the complex crocheted cables. *Well, Kate's not here*, she thought, *so I'll just have to give it another try.* She pulled out a few rows until she got back to the part she knew was right.

As she tried the stitch again and again, her mind kept wandering to the question of what else she could do to help figure out the mystery. She remembered Milt Koenig saying that his father kept an album of newspaper photos of people wearing his father's jewelry designs. She wondered if she should spend some time looking through old issues of *The Point* for photos of someone in the emeralds.

She quickly dismissed the idea. She'd spent many hours looking at back issues on other "cases." She smiled, thinking that she was starting to use detective jargon like Gwen. Annie had looked through the paper on microfiche at the library and in print copies in the newspaper's morgue of old issues. She knew exactly what kinds of photos filled the small-town paper. They were nearly all homey community events; Annie couldn't imagine anyone wearing the glitzy costume jewelry to a church auction or the Fourth of July picnic on the Town Square.

Finally, she had to admit she was getting nowhere in her musings or her crocheting. She looked ruefully at the tangled yarn and decided she needed something more physical to do, preferably something hard to mess up. She stuffed the sweater back in her project bag and headed outside to finish the raking she'd begun that morning.

Annie raked a portion of the pile of leaves onto a blue tarp, and then folded up the corners and dragged the tarp to the compost bin Wally had built for her last year. She'd had Wally put a sort of ramp up one side of the wooden bin so she could slide the tarp up the ramp and dump the load of leaves more easily into the bin. It was about the only way she could get the leaves to the bin without help.

As she dragged the tarp back, she saw an unfamiliar car pulling into the drive. It was a lovely silver Lexus. Annie recognized it as one of the new hybrids. A well-dressed man wearing sleek driving gloves stepped out of the car. "Mrs. Dawson?" he called to her.

"Yes?" Annie ran a hand through her hair, raking out a few lingering bits of leaf.

"My name is Michael Norman," he said as he strode across the lawn. "I'm Mrs. Meyer's personal assistant. She asked me to come by."

"Oh?" Annie couldn't imagine what the aloof young woman could possibly want with her that was worth sending someone out to her house.

When he reached Annie, he slipped his hand into his jacket and pulled an envelope from an inner pocket. This he handed to Annie.

Annie smiled. "You drove all the way over here to give me a note? I know the postal service can be slow, but ..."

The young man did not smile in return, though the sternness in his face did seem to soften slightly. "Mrs. Meyer thought there might be a reply."

Annie slipped an expensive sheet of creamy white paper out of the envelope. At the top of the paper, a gold embossed letter V intertwined with a silver embossed letter M.

Mrs. Dawson,

I am sorry I did not get to chat with you at the Harvest Ball, but there are always so many people to speak with. I did see you and wanted to say that you looked quite lovely.

I have decided to have the emerald earrings repaired so that I can wear them. I find the design extraordinary. Do you happen to have any more jewelry in similar design? I would love to have companion pieces to wear with the earrings. I would pay for them, of course.

Warmly,

Victoria Meyer

Annie stared at the fluid handwriting. She couldn't understand the wealthy young woman's fascination with that jewelry. She would put Mrs. Meyer at the top of her suspect list if she could distantly picture the elegant woman creeping around in the dark to snatch a hair comb or scrambling up a tree.

"Is there a reply?" Michael asked.

Annie blinked, her attention drawn back to the serious young man. "Yes," she said. "I'll need to get a pen and paper. Would you like to come in?"

"Thank you."

He followed Annie across the lawn and into the house. Just as they came through the door, Boots trotted toward them. The gray cat took one look at the stranger and puffed up angrily. She hissed and spat, stalking sideways toward them.

"Oh!" Wide-eyed, Michael backed up until he ran into the screen door. "I'm allergic to cats. I believe I'll wait on the porch." He slipped through the door and peered in at the cat, who sat glaring at him through the screen and growling.

"I'm so sorry," Annie said, wondering if she could pick up the angry cat without getting scratched. "Boots has been unusually hostile with strangers lately."

"That's quite all right," Michael said, though he took another step away from the door.

Seeing no way to reconcile man and cat, Annie hurried off to find some paper to write a note. She found a few sheets of plain pale blue paper in Gram's desk in the library and sat down to write her reply. She told Mrs. Meyer that the jewelry set had been designed by Milton Koenig and that the old man had passed away. She wrote the address and phone number of the shop in Storm Harbor. "Milton Koenig's grandson is interested in collecting pieces of his grandfather's work," Annie wrote. "I promised him any pieces I might find and wish to sell, so I would not have any to sell to you. But Mr. Koenig may be able to help you find more examples of his grandfather's work that would please you just as much. Or at least point you in the right direction to look."

Annie looked over her note. Although it seemed unlikely to make Mrs. Meyer happy, it would have to do. She slipped it into an envelope and carried it out to the anxious man on the porch.

He shifted nervously as Annie opened the door and used her foot to gently nudge Boots away to keep the cat from rushing out. The assistant nodded briefly as Annie handed him the envelope, thanked her, and hurried away to his car.

Annie looked after him for a moment, deep in thought, and then she sighed and went in search of her rake.

~ 13 ~

The next day, as Annie drove into town for the emergency mystery meeting of the Hook and Needle Club, she heard the cheerful chirp that signaled her cell phone's ringtone. She carefully pulled off the street and fished in her purse for the phone.

"Hello?"

"Mrs. Dawson? This is Milt Koenig."

"Oh, hi. Do you have news for me about the jewelry?"

"Yes, I went out to visit my parents and spent some time flipping through Dad's scrapbook. I found a photo with the necklace you brought in. Unfortunately Dad didn't clip the caption with it since it didn't mention my grandfather or the necklace."

"Oh," Annie said glumly. "I'd still like to see it."

"The photo is a little grainy, but you can make out the face of the woman wearing the gems. She doesn't look familiar, which I guess isn't that strange since I wasn't born when the photo was taken. Dad didn't know the woman's name, but he said that he seemed to remember that she was involved in some kind of big scandal. A crime or something."

Annie blinked a moment. "A crime?"

"Dad didn't know what kind. He said he remembered some kind of huge scandal, and he's sure it involved a crime. Mom didn't have any idea either."

"Did your father know when the photo might have been taken? What year?"

"I didn't ask, I'm sorry," Milt said. "He didn't volunteer it though, so he might not know. You can see most of the woman's dress. Maybe you can figure out from the style? I think women are better at that sort of thing."

Annie sighed. The more clues she found, the more muddled she felt about the whole mystery. "May I drive over and look at the picture?"

"I figured you would want to see it. Dad wouldn't give up the original, but I scanned it, and the scan came out pretty well. I can print it and mail it to you. Or I can send it by e-mail if you want."

"E-mail would be good," Annie said, crossing her fingers. She constantly had trouble with her e-mail. She wasn't really all that fond of the technological wonders of the information age. Her laptop served as a paperweight nearly as often as anything else, and she preferred doing her research at the library where someone was always around to lend a hand if the technology ever got cranky with her. She gave Milt her e-mail address, and he promised to send the photo right away.

"Thanks so much for tracking this down for me," she said. Then she told him about Mrs. Meyer and her interest in his grandfather's work. "She may be contacting you to ask about him. If you don't mind, I would prefer you didn't tell her I have the necklace and brooch. She seems to be quite a determined woman."

"No problem," he said. "Remember, you promised to keep me in mind if you decide to sell the jewelry."

"I haven't forgotten," she said. "If I sell it to anyone, it will be you. Thanks again."

She pressed the end-call button on the cell phone and tapped it thoughtfully against her chin. Someone who once owned the jewelry was involved in a crime. Still, anyone who owned the jewelry before Milt Koenig was born would be a little too old to be shinnying up trees and crawling through windows.

Again and again, Annie's mind was drawn to Mrs. Meyer's odd behavior about the jewelry. The pieces weren't all that valuable, so a wealthy woman like that wouldn't be after them for their worth. And since she couldn't be more than a few years older than Milt Koenig, she couldn't possibly be the woman in the photo.

Annie shook her head and slipped her cell phone back in her purse. Maybe the other sleuths waiting for her at A Stitch in Time could help make sense of it. She glanced at her watch and groaned, she was definitely going to be late. She pulled out carefully into the road and quickly covered the last few blocks to the needlework shop.

As she'd expected, most of the chairs were taken when she walked into the shop. Peggy was the only one missing.

"Great!" Gwen exclaimed, her eyes sparkling. "We can get started."

"You may be enjoying this far too much," Alice told her, smiling.

Gwen gave an elegant shrug. "I like a little adventure now and then."

Annie slipped into her chair. Since no one else had pulled out any needlework, she set her project bag gently on the floor beside her. "So this is strictly a mystery meeting?" she said.

"We all have updates," Alice said with a nod. "Who wants to go first?"

"I think we should start with our most obvious clue," Gwen answered. "The scratches. We need to note which of our suspects has scratches. I saw Simon Gunderson, and he has a bandaged hand, so he's still a suspect."

"For a number of reasons," Stella said primly.

"John doesn't have scratches," Alice said. "Not on his hands, forearms, neck, or face. And I don't know anyone here who could be his partner to do the housebreaking other than me."

Annie smiled. "I'll vouch for you."

"Thanks."

Kate sighed. "We haven't found Sunny to examine her for scratches, though Vanessa did find out her name from Harry. It's …"

"Sunny Day," Annie finished. "I accidentally ran into her in Storm Harbor. She has no scratches on her hands, but she was wearing a scarf around her neck that could have covered scratches."

"When I was in high school, I sometimes wore a scarf to cover … um … other things," Alice said.

Annie looked at her quizzically, not sure what she meant, and she saw equal confusion on the faces of Gwen and Stella.

"You use a scarf to cover up … um … love bites," Alice said, the last words almost a whisper.

"Oh." Annie felt her face heat up and took another peek

at Kate, who looked decidedly distressed. "Still, it could just be cat scratches."

"Or not," Kate said in a soft, sad voice. "I had to do the scarf thing in high school too. When I was dating Harry especially."

The room fell into an uneasy silence, and Annie felt horrible about making Kate feel bad. She really hadn't considered that explanation, or she might not have brought it up.

"But we can't rule this strumpet out as a suspect," Stella said, her blue eyes flashing. "That makes two suspects."

"Maybe three," Annie said quietly. "The last one doesn't really make sense, but somehow I cannot mark her off."

"Who is that?" Alice asked.

"Let me tell you what I learned from Milt Koenig first," Annie said. She explained about her meeting with the young jeweler and how he recognized the design of the remaining pieces. Then she told them about the phone call she'd gotten on the way over. "I haven't checked my e-mail yet, of course, but clearly the jewelry was made by Milt's grandfather, and a scandal may be associated with it somehow. That might be why it looked familiar to you, Stella."

Stella nodded. "It would help if I saw the photo."

"I'll bring it in after I print it out," Annie said.

"But that doesn't tell us who the new suspect is," Kate said. "Surely you don't think it's someone Stella's age, climbing trees and grabbing jewelry."

"No, but someone *has* shown an enduring fascination with this set of jewelry." Annie went on to describe the mask auction and the unusual change in Victoria Meyer's behavior. "She paid a thousand dollars for the little mask I made, but then she didn't wear it at the ball."

"The mask she wore matched her gown perfectly," Gwen said. "I noticed it because I remembered how much her husband paid for it. It *is* possible she didn't know he'd bought it when he did."

"But my mask would have never gone well with that gown," Annie said.

"A woman like Victoria Meyer has many gowns," Stella said. "Choosing a different one is a small matter."

Annie nodded. "I know, and that makes perfect sense, except she sent her assistant to my house to try to buy the rest of the set."

"She knew there was more to the set?" Alice asked, her eyebrows raised.

"I'm not sure," Annie said. "Her note was vague. She was interested if there was more to the set. Maybe I'm just being silly."

"I really can't picture that woman climbing trees," Alice said.

"But a woman like that could easily hire someone to climb trees for her," Stella said, coloring slightly as she spoke. "As much as I loathe bringing up my own foolish mistakes of the past, I did hire someone to retrieve something from Annie once."

Annie smiled gently at her. "All water well under the bridge."

Gwen cocked her head and asked, "Stella, do you think Victoria is a suspect?"

Stella sighed. "I don't know, but I am merely saying we shouldn't automatically dismiss her out of hand. I fully know that money and position do not keep a woman from behaving foolishly."

"I'll concede that," Gwen said. "But I still think those two biologists are involved in this. Their behavior is just as odd. The young man clearly has the scratches. And either one of them is fully capable of climbing trees or grabbing hair combs!"

Mary Beth crossed her arms and leaned back in her chair. "I'll concede that Jenna Paige is a bit overwhelming, but she hasn't done anything ominous."

"So, did you learn anything new about her when she came into the shop yesterday?" Annie said. "Gwen told me Stella planned to grill her."

"She doesn't require much grilling," Mary Beth said mildly. "With Miss Paige it's more a matter of directing the flow."

"She continues to ask a great many questions about the community," Stella said. "All completely unrelated to lobsters and lobster fishing. Yesterday, she asked me about the Historical Society, the cultural center, Dress to Impress, and the public school system." The old woman sniffed slightly. "I cannot imagine why she would think I know anything about the local public school system. I am hardly likely to be the parent of small children."

"Did you manage to ask her anything?" Alice asked.

"It wasn't easy," Stella said. "But I did direct the conversation to the Harvest Ball, and I learned where those ridiculous costumes came from, which of the dresses she liked best at the ball, and her opinion of each of the canapés that Maplehurst Inn served."

"Not exactly related to the theft," Alice said.

Stella held up a hand. "I also heard her lengthy opinion about the electrical wiring at Maplehurst Inn and how it might cause a blackout. Apparently Dr. Gunderson is quite good at electrical wiring, and he is especially interested in old buildings."

"And would likely know how to turn off the lights in an old inn," Alice said.

"Likely so," Stella said. "I also learned that as soon as the lights went out, Dr. Gunderson left, telling her he was going to see if he could help with the power problem. She was quite proud of him for his helpfulness, even if it left her without a dance partner for over an hour."

"See," Gwen said. "He has the knowledge to put out the lights. He left Jenna in the dark and didn't reappear until after he'd had plenty of time to get to Annie's and back."

"It also sounds like Jenna is not involved," Mary Beth noted. "She'd hardly tell you all that if she knew how suspicious it looked."

"Maybe not," Gwen said doubtfully, "but you have to admit this boosts Simon Gunderson to the top of the suspect list."

"But why?" Annie asked. "The jewels aren't valuable. Why steal them?"

"Maybe they thought they were valuable?" Kate said with a shrug. "When you showed us the rest of the set, I thought they looked real. Not everyone can recognize what's real or not in jewelry."

"But wouldn't jewel thieves need to know?" Annie asked. "If you steal jewelry for a living, you'd probably know jewelry."

"Unless you're simply grabbing something because you liked it," Mary Beth said. "Which puts Sunny Day in the lead as far as I'm concerned."

"She definitely didn't seem like the brightest bulb in the chandelier," Alice said. "I could see her as being impulsive."

"But leaving the ball and breaking into my house doesn't sound all that impulsive," Annie responded.

"Sounds greedy," Mary Beth responded. "And I can totally picture her being greedy."

Alice raised an eyebrow. "You haven't even met her."

"I know enough about her." Mary Beth recrossed her arms as if the matter were settled for her. Annie suspected Mary Beth's firmness was as much from loyalty to Kate as from any kind of logic.

"Maybe that biologist is connected to the scandal somehow," Gwen said, clearly intent on keeping her favorite suspects in the lead. "Maybe the original owner was Simon Gunderson's grandmother or something, and he's swiping them back for her."

"I don't know that we're going to come any closer to solving the mystery at this point," Annie said. "We need to know more. I'll get the photo from Milt Koenig, and we'll see if we can learn the identity of the woman in it."

"And find out if she's Simon Gunderson's grandmother," Gwen said.

"And find out who she is," Annie corrected. "And what scandal was connected to her."

"That makes sense," Alice said. "So is the sleuthing meeting over? I need to pop into The Cup & Saucer to catch Peggy up on everything." She turned to Annie. "Want to come?"

Annie sighed. "If you don't mind waiting just a few more minutes." She turned to Kate. "I'm totally stuck on that cable stitch in the sweater sleeves. Can you help me?"

Kate smiled at her warmly. "Of course."

While Kate began unraveling the mystery of the crochet cable for Annie, the rest of the Stony Point sleuths slowly drifted out of the store, promising to report back if they learned anything else. Alice stood at the counter and chatted with Mary Beth as she waited on Annie.

With Kate's sure hands demonstrating the cable stitch and twists, Annie quickly saw what she was doing wrong. "Sometimes a technique is really easy once you see how it's done," Kate said, "etven though the instructions seem complicated."

Annie worked a few rows while Kate watched, just to be certain she had it. She then gave Kate a quick thank-you hug and packed the sweater in her project bag. "I'm ready," she told Alice.

"Great, I could really use a nice jolt of caffeine," Alice admitted.

Annie looked closely at her friend as they walked out of the shop. Alice looked tired. The laugh lines that gave her face much of its mischievous look seemed deeper, making her look older. "Are you feeling all right?" she asked.

"I'm exhausted," Alice said. "I had trouble falling asleep last night. All this business with John brings back a past I

* Sorry, can't help it. ☺

really don't like revisiting."

"I'm sorry," Annie said. "Do you think he'll be leaving soon?"

"I'd like to hope so, but I think it'll take a while to get my footing back even then. It's like having the stupidest thing you've ever done pushed right in your face ... coupled with all these memories of some really bad times."

Annie nodded. She couldn't really know how Alice felt, but she couldn't begin to imagine how much it would have hurt if Wayne had ever betrayed her trust, or if she'd found out what she'd believed about him was a lie. In some ways, it might have been even worse than the pain of losing him after a long, wonderful marriage.

Alice gave her a light shoulder bump. "I'll be all right. I promise."

"I'll hold you to that."

They settled down to a pleasant cup of coffee at the diner, catching Peggy up on what had happened at the meeting in small bits so that her boss wouldn't yell at her for spending too long a time at their table. It became almost a game, seeing how much they could pack into a coffee refill, and soon all three were giggling over it.

Finally Peggy said, "OK, I think I'm caught up now."

"Good," Annie said. "If I drank one more refill, I don't think I'd be able to sleep for the rest of the week."

"I am feeling a little fidgety," Alice admitted as they paid the check and left the diner. "I think I'll work some of the nervous energy off with some shopping. Want to come?"

"I don't think so," Annie said. "But you have fun."

Alice smiled. "I plan to."

Annie watched her friend climb into her sporty convertible and pull out, the breeze already tugging her auburn hair as she waved back at Annie. Annie hoped a little shopping therapy would help bring back a little of the Alice-spirit she knew and loved.

~ 14 ~

The next morning, Annie decided to have a little electronic sleuthing with her morning coffee. She hauled her laptop and the tiny portable printer downstairs to the kitchen to check her e-mail and finally see the mystery woman. As she sorted out what to plug in and where, she was reminded again why she normally did research at the public library. She really just preferred to work with computers in a place where she had someone to call for help.

The laptop had been a birthday present from LeeAnn a couple of years earlier. LeeAnn had gushed about how she could send photos of the twins, but her busy daughter had as little time for e-mail as Annie had inclination.

Still, she'd followed LeeAnn's orders about getting Internet through the cable company, just in case she needed it. She just hoped the little blinking cable modem was letting her connect because she had no idea what to do if it decided to be contrary.

She nearly clapped when messages began to appear in her e-mail program. Since she hadn't touched the computer in weeks, she had to wait as a variety of messages offering her discount medicines from Canada, untold wealth from Nigeria, and the names of swinging singles in her area. She shuddered as she deleted these without opening them.

Finally the e-mail from Koenig's Jewelry popped up and

Annie held her breath while she clicked on it. Would the photo help her solve this mystery? She scanned Milt's brief note. It basically said the same things he'd told her on the phone. Then she double-clicked the attachment.

A photo filled her screen. It showed a slightly grainy black-and-white newspaper photo of a dark-haired woman laughing. The woman wore a dark dress and a fur wrap. Peeking from the gap between the edges of the fur wrap, Annie could clearly see the emerald necklace. Behind the woman in the photo stood a man with light-color hair, but so little of him showed that Annie wouldn't have recognized him even if she'd known him.

Annie stared at the woman's open-mouthed laugh. She seemed so carefree and happy. At the same time, her carefully styled hair and the fur wrap definitely suggested money. But did she look like any of Annie's suspects?

Annie shook her head. There just was no way to judge any kind of resemblance from the photo. Certainly she didn't look enough like anyone to trigger recognition. With a sigh, she sent the photo to the printer, hoping that Stella might find the woman more familiar.

After she tucked the printed photo in her cardigan pocket, Annie decided to use her own coffee-induced energy to finish the raking, not that raking could truly be called "finished" as long as so many leaves still hung from the trees. Still, she found the raking and hauling a good way to use her hands as her mind wandered from suspect to suspect.

As Annie heaved the last tarp load of leaves into her compost bin, she heard the sound of tires on gravel and turned to see another strange car pull into her driveway.

She squinted into the low sun to see if she could identify the driver.

The car stopped and she immediately recognized the tall man who climbed out. Frowning, she wondered what John MacFarlane wanted with her.

"Good afternoon," he said pleasantly as he walked toward her.

Annie was suddenly sorry she'd finished her raking. She'd probably enjoy seeing the perfectly pressed cuff of his pants fill up with leaves. "What can I do for you?" she asked.

"I went by Alice's, but she wasn't home," he said. "Do you know when she'll be back?"

Annie shook her head. "Alice doesn't check in with me."

"That's not what I hear," he said, folding his arms cross his chest.

"Oh?"

"It seems to me you have a great deal of influence with Alice," he said, and suddenly the smooth charm she'd seen every time she spoke with him slipped away. "I have to wonder why you're so intent on her not getting back together with me."

"Alice makes her own decisions about you."

"So you're not going to admit you don't want to see us together."

"I don't want to see Alice hurt," Annie said. "She's my friend. But she's also an adult, and she makes her own decisions just fine."

"Except that here in Stony Point with her old friend Annie, she suddenly doesn't trust me. She suddenly doesn't want to see me."

Annie stared at him in disbelief. "You don't think cheating on her and dumping her in a world of debt had anything to do with that?"

"So you two *do* talk about me?" His smile was as cold as the chill that slid up Annie's back.

"We talk about most things that bother us," Annie said, "but I'm really not interested in discussing Alice or our friendship with you. It seems to me that Alice is handling you just fine."

He took a step closer, crowding Annie's personal space. "Don't make me show you how I handle things that bother me, Annie Dawson."

Annie reached behind her and wrapped a fist around the rake handle, she brought it around her body quickly and pushed the end into John's stomach slightly. "You need to leave," she said. "We've got nothing else to talk about."

He looked down at the rake handle, then back up into her face. "For now."

He took a step back, and then he turned and walked quickly back to his car. Annie drew in a deep, shaky breath. He may not be a suspect in her break-in, but something told Annie that John MacFarlane could definitely be a dangerous man.

Annie put her rake and tarp away, but she jumped at any sound in the driveway, and finally she accepted that John had truly frightened her. She went inside and carefully locked the door behind her.

She wondered if she should tell anyone about their confrontation. He hadn't exactly threatened her, though he had certainly been menacing. He hadn't waved a weapon around, and he hadn't even touched her. She was the one who poked him with a rake handle. He'd frightened her, but it didn't seem like anything she should bring to Chief Edwards. Her last conversation with the chief had left her feeling slightly foolish, and she didn't want to repeat that.

She could tell Ian, of course. He definitely wouldn't brush aside her concerns, especially since he didn't like John in the first place. But she worried that he might over-react a little. She certainly didn't want to be the cause of some kind of macho confrontation where either man got hurt. She didn't like John—and she desperately wanted him to leave Stony Point—but she didn't want to provoke Ian to go after him either.

Annie picked up the phone and began to dial Alice's cell. Then she stopped and hung up. Alice looked so tired from all this business with her ex. Annie didn't want to make it worse, and Alice would definitely feel guilty if she knew John had frightened Annie.

As she sat at the edge of the chair, staring at the phone, Boots padded into the room and rubbed against her ankles. Annie scooped the cat up and gave her a gentle hug. "Some-one scared me a little, Boots," she said. Boots responded by rubbing Annie's chin with her head.

She held the soft, warm cat for some time, petting her until Annie felt calmer and more in control of herself. John MacFarlane had been trying to intimidate her, and it had worked. But now she felt more in control of herself. She even smiled a little as she remembered Betsy Holden's no-nonsense advice about fear.

"Fear only has one job," Gram told her. "It's supposed to

point you at places you need to be careful. When you find that fear is getting a little too big for its britches, you have to put it in its place. Tell it that you're going to be careful, and after that just tell it to shut up! You're the one who's in charge of what goes on inside of you—don't ever forget that."

"Right, Gram," Annie said softly. She'd be careful of John MacFarlane, but she wasn't going to cower and shake. With that, she looked down and realized Boots had fallen asleep in her arms. She carried the sleeping cat to the sofa and laid her gently on the soft cushions.

Annie decided she didn't want to simply sit at home and fret about the mystery, and certainly not about John's threats. Since it was Saturday night, she decided to drive into town and see if Mary Beth or perhaps another friend might want to go to dinner with her. A little company was sure to give her some perspective. Plus, stopping by A Stitch in Time might give her a chance to show the photo of the woman to Stella, since the older woman often came into the needlework shop during the week to spend some time knitting and chatting with Mary Beth and Kate.

As Annie pulled into a parking space between A Stitch in Time and the diner, she was delighted to see the shiny white Lincoln Continental that she knew was Stella Brickson's car. *Stella must be knitting at the shop*, Annie thought as she climbed out of her own car, trying not to notice how much her burgundy Malibu could use a nice wash, especially compared to Stella's spotless vehicle.

Annie walked to the big window that covered much of the front of A Stitch in Time and peeked in. She saw Mary

Beth deep in conversation with a customer as they stood huddled together near one of the yarn cubbies. Annie's gaze swept the rest of the shop, but she didn't see Stella.

Frowning, Annie stepped away from the shop. Should she go in and ask if Mary Beth had seen Stella? Surely the elderly woman hadn't walked far from the car. Annie looked up and down the sidewalk, finally spotting a figure she recognized. Stella's driver Jason was walking away from her, carrying what seemed to be a heavy cardboard box. She hurried to catch up with him. "Jason?"

He turned and smiled at her. "Mrs. Dawson."

"Is Stella in town?" she asked.

"No, not today," he said, and then he dropped his voice and leaned closer to her. "It's a dread secret, but she's caught a cold. She never likes it to get around when she has something so common." He laughed lightly.

"Oh, I was hoping to show her something," she said.

He shrugged apologetically, and Annie heard something shift in the box. "I shouldn't be keeping you here chatting. The box looks heavy."

"It's just some dishes Mrs. Brickson loaned the Historical Society for the ball," he said. "They ran short, and Mrs. Brickson had the same pattern in abundance. The Bricksons could have hosted a dinner party for fifty and all the china would've matched."

"Now that would be quite an undertaking," Annie said. "Well, I would tell you to pass along get-well wishes, but since her cold is a secret, I'll just keep a good thought."

"That'll do," he said cheerfully. "You have a nice day now." Then he strode past her with the heavy box.

So much for finding out who the woman in the photo might be, Annie thought, frustrated. She wondered if it would be worth carrying the photo to the Historical Society. She doubted Liz Booth missed much that went on around Stony Point, but the slightly prim president of the Historical Society had made her feelings about gossip pretty clear back when Annie and Alice had been trying to solve a mystery about a tattered rag doll.

Annie felt at loose ends until she saw Ian Butler crossing the street toward her with a smile on his face. "I'm very glad to see you," he said. "I was going to search for meat to soothe the savage beast. Would you like to join me for dinner?"

Annie smiled slightly. "I don't know. I've probably seen enough savage beasts today."

"Oh?"

She waved her hand lightly. "Never mind. So shall we go to the diner?"

"I'm not sure I'm in the mood for the diner tonight," he said. "Would you mind if we go to the inn? They make a fantastic venison stew this time of year, and I've been thinking about it all day."

Annie looked anxiously down the street. John MacFarlane was staying at the inn, and she definitely did not want to run into him again. Then she remembered Alice saying John wouldn't eat at the inn because of the expense. "OK," she said tentatively.

"Annie, are you all right?" Ian asked.

She nodded and forced a smile. "It's just been a bit of a long, weird day."

"I insist that you tell me all about it," he said as he put a hand at her back to coax her down the sidewalk toward the inn.

"It's not really worth talking about." Then she slipped the folded photo out of her pocket and handed it to Ian. "Do you recognize this woman?"

Ian looked it over and shook his head. "It looks like an older photo, though. I doubt this woman has looked like this for a long time. She probably looks like Stella now."

Annie nodded glumly and slipped the paper back in her pocket. "I'll just have to try to be patient until I can show it to Stella."

They walked along in friendly silence for a bit until they reached the movie theater. Annie glanced at the ghoulish movie posters on display and shuddered. "I can't imagine why anyone would sit through a movie that involves chopping people up," she said.

"You probably have to be a teenage boy," he said mildly, glancing at the posters. "I suspect it might have something to do with scaring your date into clinging to you in the dark."

Annie laughed lightly. "I saw a few movies while clinging to Wayne's arm," Annie admitted, "but none of them had so much gore. I wanted to be able to eat my popcorn!"

"Sounds like a sensible approach," Ian said. "Though I do like to go to the movies now and then. I like action flicks." He stopped and pointed at a poster that showed Bruce Willis and several other older action stars striding purposefully toward them. "That one I would watch."

Annie looked it over skeptically. "Do you suppose they cut people up?"

"Not likely," he said. "But there might be explosions. Lots of explosions." Then he grinned boyishly. "At least I hope so."

"I bet you watch that *MythBusters* show on television," Annie said.

"How did you know?"

"Because every time I see a commercial for it, something is blowing up."

Ian chuckled warmly, and they walked the rest of the way to the inn as Ian recited a list of the things he'd seen blown up in the name of science television.

The sidewalk curved around to the front of the inn. The wide porch was still bright with Annie's donated mums, and she enjoyed the cheery sight of them.

Inside, they were quickly led to a cozy table, spread with a crisp, white cloth. Ian barely glanced at the menu before ordering a bowl of venison stew. Annie chose grilled salmon.

"Not in the mood to eat Bambi?" Ian teased lightly.

"No, I like venison," Annie said. "Though I have to admit I don't think I could shoot a deer. I love it when I see deer in the yard at Grey Gables. I don't even mind that I have to plant my spring flowers over and over. But for eating, I like salmon better."

The food at the inn was delicious, and Ian's company soon made the stress of the day and the mystery slip away. Annie was glad she'd left the house and not spent the evening fretting.

"So, will you tell me now what was bothering you before?" Ian asked as they sipped after-dinner coffee.

"Just an unpleasant encounter with someone," Annie

said with a smile. "I guess I'm always surprised when I can't get along with everyone."

"That surprises me too," Ian said, but he didn't badger to know more.

She appreciated that Ian seemed willing to respect her limits, both in conversation and in their relationship. She wasn't quite sure what their relationship was. She had to admit that going to the ball and having dinner in the beautifully decorated inn certainly looked like dates. She thought back to the karaoke dinner at Sweet Nell's when Ian serenaded her. It was no wonder her friends teased her and gave her knowing smiles. But they didn't really feel like dates. Annie's heart belonged to Wayne; maybe it always would. But she was certainly glad for Ian's friendship.

When they finished and walked out into the inn's entry, Annie was startled to see John MacFarlane striding through the front doors. She froze. Ian looked from Annie to John quizzically. John had also stopped, and he smiled at Annie and Ian, flashing bright white teeth like a dog baring its fangs.

"Good evening, Mr. MacFarlane," Ian said.

"Good evening, Mr. Mayor," John responded. "Nice night to be out with a pretty lady. I'm glad to see you enjoying yourself, Mrs. Dawson."

Annie didn't respond, and she saw Ian's gaze shift between them again.

"So, will you be leaving Stony Point soon?" Ian asked.

"I hope so. Though I'm staying until my business here is done, and I get what I need."

"That sounds ominous," Ian said. "I hope you know

how important this town and *all* its residents are to me, Mr. MacFarlane."

John smiled his wolfish smile. "Sometimes you can keep your residents safe best by being sure they aren't getting involved in things that don't concern them."

Ian's eyes narrowed. "I don't like the sound of that at all."

"I'm not surprised." With that, John MacFarlane simply stepped around them and walked on toward the stairs that led up to the rooms.

"Annie, would you care to tell me what all that was about?"

"I'd rather not."

"If he's threatened you," Ian said, "or threatened Alice, I want to know. I can't help if you keep me locked out."

Annie continued on out the door, letting the evening air cool her flushed face. "He thinks I'm influencing Alice. He thinks that's why she told him she doesn't want anything to do with him."

"How do you know that?"

"He came by Grey Gables today."

Ian stiffened, glancing back toward the inn door. Annie was pretty sure that if Ian were a cat, his hair would be standing on end, and he'd be growling. She put a hand on his arm. "I don't really think I have anything to worry about. He tried to bully me a little, yes, but I would rather you didn't do anything. Not without talking to Alice. I don't want to do anything that makes all this worse for her."

Ian's scowl softened. "I've never met anyone who thinks about others as much as you do, Annie Dawson. But sometimes, it's all right to think about *you* some too."

"I'm not nearly as selfless as you think," she said. "If I really need you, I promise to scream."

~ 15 ~

The next morning dawned warm and clear, so Annie carried her morning coffee out on the porch with a pad and pen. She'd decided to try making a list of suspects and the clues she knew about each. Maybe it would turn out to be like one of those puzzles where once you sorted out all the clues, you knew exactly who the culprit was.

After a lot of writing and sipping, Annie ended up with an empty mug and no real idea who had stolen her hair comb.

"You look frustrated!"

Annie looked up, startled. She'd been so deep in thought she hadn't noticed Alice striding across the lawn with one of her wonderful breakfast treats. "I was trying to look at our mystery like a logic puzzle," she said.

"Doesn't look like it's going well," Alice said. "But I might have an idea."

"Great!" Annie stood up. "Bring your idea on inside, and I'll get us some coffee to go with whatever you have wrapped up there."

"Pumpkin, applesauce, cream-cheese muffins," Alice said. "They're delicious if you try not to think about the calories."

They were soon seated in their usual spots in the cozy kitchen cradling warm mugs. Annie took a bite of soft, steamy muffin and moaned. "Whatever your idea is, I love it just because of these muffins."

Alice laughed. "In that case, I'm definitely making some of these for my next Divine Décor party. I am totally open to taking unfair advantage where I can."

As soon as Annie could talk without her mouth being full, she asked what Alice's idea was.

"Well, even though I gave up on my primary suspect," Alice said. "I still want to be part of the investigation, and I thought of the perfect thing to do next. We should go over to the inn tomorrow and find out exactly why the lights went out at the ball. Surely they know by now."

Annie blinked at her. "That does make sense." Then she felt a little uneasy shiver creep up her spine. She really did not want to run into Alice's ex again. Twice in one day was far more than enough.

"What's wrong?" Alice said immediately.

Annie frowned. "I'm beginning to suspect I'm entirely too easy to read."

"We've been friends for a long time," Alice said. "And … actually, you *are* easy to read. That's why we never could get away with anything."

"Oh sure, blame me," Annie said. "It couldn't be because your crazy ideas made adults suspicious all the time."

Alice smiled over the top of her coffee cup but merely said, "So what's wrong?"

Annie sighed and gave in. She told Alice about her two recent encounters with John MacFarlane. By the time she was done, Alice's face was flushed and her brows were drawn together.

"I probably earned part of that," she said with a sigh. "I did become a doormat when I was with John. I don't know how it happened. A little at a time, I suppose. But I guess he thought I'd just fall back into old habits and let him tell me what to do."

"If I had any doubts about him being bad for you," Annie said, "just knowing that relationship made *you* act like that is proof enough to me."

Alice nodded. "I really didn't like myself very much then." She looked at Annie seriously. "But I'm not going back to being like that."

"I'm glad to hear it."

"I don't think you need to be scared of John," Alice said. "He can be a bit of a bully, but even at our worst times he never got physical."

Annie just nodded.

"Anyway, let's talk about the plan," Alice said. "You want to go over to the inn with me on Monday morning? We can ask Linda about the electricity."

"Linda?"

"Linda Hunter, she owns the inn. You haven't met?"

"No, but I'm looking forward to it."

They chatted a few more minutes, and then the two friends parted so they could each get ready for church. Annie invited Alice to come over after the service for dinner, but Alice grinned sheepishly.

"I promised to update Peggy on our plans," she admitted, "so I'll be hitting the diner after church. Do you want to come with me?"

Annie shook her head. "I've eaten out enough. I think

I'll stay home and work on my crocheting. I might even have it figured out after Kate's last tutorial."

The day turned out to be pleasantly mystery-free, but Annie found she was quite eager to get back on the trail of the mystery when Monday morning dawned sunny and cool. The sooner they figured out what was going on, the sooner she'd feel really confident again.

When the phone rang, Annie hurried across the room to grab it, hoping it wasn't Alice canceling their sleuthing expedition. She smiled when she recognized her daughter's breathless voice. "John, take that critter outside right this minute!"

"Frog?" Annie asked.

"Maybe—I'm not sure," LeeAnn responded. "But I definitely saw legs and wiggling. Hi, Mom—do you have any more of that fabric?"

It took Annie a moment to think back to their last conversation and the fabric Annie had sent for Joanna's trick-or-treat costume. "I don't think so," Annie said, "but I could check Gram's closet. I seem to remember some cloth amongst the stuff dragged out of her closet during the break-in, though I'm not sure if there is any more of that print."

"Break-in!" LeeAnn yelped. "What happened this time?"

"I don't know how on earth I let that slip out!" Annie said. "It's nothing you need to worry about."

"Easy for you to say when you're a billion miles away," her daughter scolded. "Now tell me everything and don't leave out a word."

Annie ran through the short version of the loss of the hair comb and the break-in. "We don't know that they're connected," she said. "And nothing has really happened since. Nothing was stolen. Mostly I just had to do a little cleaning up."

"I'm more concerned that nothing was stolen," LeeAnn said. "It sounds like someone was looking for that jewelry. Maybe you should go ahead and sell it to the jeweler. You could make a big deal about it. Then everyone would know not to bother you anymore."

Annie thought about that and a vague idea seemed to be suggested by LeeAnn's words. Maybe she wouldn't do exactly what her daughter said, but she could see how something like that would possibly be a good idea. If the thief thought she was about to sell the pieces, maybe they could use that to force the thief's hand and lure him or her into a trap.

"Hello? ... Earth calling Mom," LeeAnn said. "Are you there, Mom?"

Annie realized she'd tuned out her daughter, "Sorry, sweetheart, your idea about selling the jewelry sounds like a good one."

"Good." LeeAnn sounded pleased. "Now, back to the fabric. Could you take a quick peek? I am just the tiniest smidge short. If you had just enough for a dress sleeve, I can make Joanna's outfit match the doll exactly. Otherwise, I'm going to have to do contrast sleeves, and your granddaughter has already informed me that they won't match properly if I do that."

"Well, knowing exactly what she wants sounds like a trait she inherited from someone else I know," Annie said.

LeeAnn laughed. "OK, I can be a *little* bit that way. But will you check?"

"Sure, I'll check right now," Annie carried the handset to Gram's bedroom and poked around in the closet with one hand while she held the phone in the other. Annie brought the conversation around to Thanksgiving while she searched.

"Herb is weakening," LeeAnn said. "I still can't promise, but I think he's going to cave. I *am* getting kind of excited about the idea of coming to Stony Point. At the very least, I can keep you from getting involved in a new mystery while I'm there."

"I don't know," Annie said. "I think you would like the mysteries a lot more if you were involved too."

"You might have a point."

"Hey, I found some," Annie said, pulling out a length of fabric sandwiched between two others. "There is definitely enough here for the sleeve."

"Excellent," LeeAnn said. "Can you overnight that? I'm a desperate woman."

Annie promised and carried the fabric to the front room where she stuffed it into her project bag. She'd buy an Express Mail envelope and postage at the post office to mail it out.

"Annie?" Alice called out as she came through the front door, tapping on the door frame lightly.

"Right here," Annie sent her love to the twins and quickly ended the call with her daughter.

Annie spotted the Divine Décor catalog tucked in Alice's purse. When Annie raised her eyebrows, Alice said, "What? Linda is a customer. I'll just be killing two birds with one visit!"

"I didn't say anything," Annie said.

"It was all over your face," Alice answered.

Annie held up her hands. "I'm totally innocent."

"Sure," Alice said. "Should we ride together or take separate cars?"

"We can go together if you don't mind the post office stop," Annie said. "My car or yours?"

"Let's take mine. It's a gorgeous day, and I won't get to drive with the top down for much longer this year."

"Sounds good," Annie said. "Just don't let me forget to stop at the post office while we're in town."

Annie agreed after grabbing a scarf to cover her hair, and they headed out. The normally boisterous breeze was unusually still, and the sun felt deliciously warm as they climbed into Alice's little convertible. Once they got going though, they had plenty of wind whipping their hair around.

When they pulled up in the half-round circle, they were both laughing from the sheer joy of the ride. After the tension of the last few days, Annie felt refreshed from the laughter, as if the wind had whipped away her worries in addition to mussing her hair.

Inside the inn, Annie felt a flash of nerves, but when she didn't see Alice's ex, the flutter settled down quickly. They crossed the dark, well-worn wood floor quickly to reach the front desk. "Is Linda around?" Alice asked.

The wide-eyed girl nodded. "Yes, ma'am. Just a moment." She ducked through a door behind the desk.

Alice leaned closer to Annie and whispered, "I hate being *ma'amed*."

"You'd better never move to Texas. I started getting

called 'ma'am' when I was twenty-one. It was horrifying."

Linda Hunter, a slender woman with salt-and-pepper hair cut into a bob, hurried through the door. When she caught sight of Alice, she smiled. "Alice! It's nice to see you. Rachel thought you were reporters."

"Reporters?" Alice echoed.

"*New England Country Inns* magazine is doing a feature on historic buildings, and they're sending a photographer and writer out. They're not due until this afternoon so Rachel was panicking a little."

"Then we're catching you at a bad time," Alice said.

"I have a minute." The woman turned her warm smile toward Annie, and Alice quickly introduced them. "Oh, I've heard of you," the innkeeper said, looking concerned. "Someone took your hair comb at the ball. I'm so sorry about that. Is that why you're here?"

"Not exactly," Annie said. "I certainly don't blame you about the hair comb, and it wasn't particularly valuable."

A look of relief passed over the woman's face.

"We're actually here to ask you about the lights going out at the ball," Alice said. "Did you ever find out why they went out?"

Linda sighed. "Someone's idea of a joke, I suppose. Someone had switched off the main. It shut off power all over the inn. You wouldn't believe the number of complaints I got over that. There were even a couple of minor injuries. It's a good thing I'm insured."

"Oh my," Annie said. "I didn't know anyone was hurt."

"One of the guests ran into a door in her room and received a black eye," Linda said as she ticked things off on her fingers. "One of our cooks was burned slightly on one hand. And our handyman turned an ankle, apparently someone else went downstairs to check on the main too, and they ran into each other on the stairs."

"Really?" Alice said. "Who was the other person?"

"I never found out. I figured it was a member of the waitstaff. The person was probably afraid he'd get in trouble, though I certainly don't blame people for accidents. I try to be very fair with my employees."

"I know you do," Alice said. She glanced over at Annie, and Annie knew they were both thinking the same thing—whoever had shut off the lights probably ran into the handyman.

"Could we speak with your handyman?" Alice asked.

"Sure, if you would like to." The innkeeper lowered her voice. "Is this about one of those mysteries you told me about, Alice?"

Alice nodded, and a grin spread across Linda's face. "How exciting! Promise you'll tell me how it turns out?"

"I will," Alice said. "So, the handyman?"

"Oh, right. Richard's actually down in the cellar checking out the Christmas decorations to see what still works, and what we'll need to replace." She glanced at her watch, and then turned to the young clerk. "Can you show these ladies to the cellar door, Rachel? I'm expecting a couple of people for job interviews. I never get a slow moment."

"Thanks for your help," Alice said. Then she passed over the Divine Décor catalog she'd brought. "I wanted to give you the new catalog too."

"Oh, great. Does it have holiday things yet?"

"Of course."

The other woman immediately began leafing through the catalog as Annie and Alice followed Rachel. She took them through the dining room, and then the kitchen. The door to the cellar was at the back of the kitchen storeroom.

"Do I need to come down with you?" she asked hesitantly. "The cellar creeps me out."

"No, we'll be fine," Annie answered, patting the girl on the arm. Rachel quickly hurried off as Annie and Alice headed down the narrow wooden stairs to the cellar.

Annie turned to Alice as they walked and asked, "Do you know this fellow?"

Alice nodded. "Richard Bent. He's a nice guy."

They reached the bottom and looked around. The cellar was a maze of cement walls and dim lighting. "I can see why this gives that girl the creeps," Alice said, then she raised her voice. "Richard? Are you down here?"

"Over here," a man's voice answered. "Who's there?"

Alice and Annie followed the voice, coming to a fairly large room lined with deep shelves. Dusty cardboard boxes filled the shelves, except for the few that lay on the floor, their contents partially emptied. In the middle of the disarray, a tall, thin man in jeans and a baggy brown henley shirt was standing over a wire-frame reindeer, plugging in the lights that were strung around the reindeer's frame.

Like the innkeeper, he smiled brightly at Alice. "Hello! It's not often I get visited by lovely ladies while I'm in the bowels of the Maplehurst. How can I help you?"

Alice quickly introduced him to Annie. "We wanted to ask you about the person who bumped into you on the stairs when the lights were out at the ball."

"Oh, I didn't see the guy," Richard said. "I was using my cell phone for a flashlight, and it's pretty dark down here when the lights are *on*, so you can imagine what it's like by cell-phone glow."

"But you know it was a man?" Annie said.

"Oh, yeah, I saw him that well before he knocked the phone out of my hand. Plus, he ran into me pretty hard. I'd have known if it had been a woman."

"Do you remember any details about him at all?" Annie asked.

Richard paused, thinking a moment. "Well, he had his head ducked, so I couldn't see his face. His hair looked dark, but that could have been from the poor lighting. Anything less than snow-white hair would look dark, I think. It was hard to judge his height, but I don't think he was short. And we both could fit on the stairs, so he couldn't have been fat. Does that help at all? Why do you want to know anyway?"

"Someone stole a hair comb from Annie in the dark," Alice said. "We're just wondering if the guy you ran into might have been the one who turned out the lights."

Richard shrugged. "Hard to say. I figured it was some-one trying to turn the lights back on." He gestured around the cellar. "It's hard to find anything down here, so if one of the waiters or cooks had come down, wanting to be helpful, he probably couldn't have found the fuse box."

"Well, thanks for your time," Annie said.

"No problem," Richard said. "It's nice to have the break. I'm getting really tired of Rudolph here. He's Linda's favorite, but I can't get him to light up." Then he shrugged.

"Oh well, back to making Christmas magic."

"Good luck," Alice said.

Annie and Alice walked back through the dusty cellar and headed upstairs. "So did we learn anything useful?" Alice asked.

"We know that whoever took the hair comb is not the person who turned out the lights," Annie said. "If Richard ran into the man on the steps, that person couldn't have been upstairs grabbing my hair comb. He'd have to be in two places at once."

"So that leaves out John again," Alice said.

Annie nodded. "And it means Sunny could only have done it if Harry was willing to go turn out the lights for her. I really can't see them pulling off something like this. I know Harry has done some unfortunate things, but that just seems ridiculous."

"You could argue that for anyone," Alice responded. "Why go to so much trouble for a piece of jewelry that probably wouldn't sell for more than a hundred dollars on a good day?"

Annie shook her head. Then she stopped suddenly, causing Alice to bump into her. As she looked across the inn's lobby, she couldn't believe her eyes.

～ 16 ～

Coming out of the door behind the front desk, Annie recognized Sunny Day walking beside Linda Hunter. Then Annie remembered her conversation with the young woman at the dark restaurant in Storm Harbor. Apparently Sunny had made good on her plan to try for a better job at Maplehurst Inn.

"What's the matter?" Alice whispered.

"That young woman," Annie replied softly. "That's Sunny Day, Harry's date for the ball."

Alice looked over at the younger woman. "Well, she's not wearing a scarf," she said. "We could check for cat-scratch scars."

Just then, Sunny glanced in their direction and spotted Annie. She said some final thing to Linda, and then she hurried over. "Oh, hello! I did it! I got a job here." She stopped and looked around. "It's not quite as fancy as it was at that party, but it has to be better than that dump I've been working in."

"It's definitely better lit," Annie said mildly.

Sunny giggled. "Yep, which means I won't have to check the food for wildlife before I carry it to the table."

That thought made Annie feel queasy, but very glad she hadn't ordered any food at the dark restaurant. She could see Sunny's neck plainly with the young woman's low-cut blouse and though there were some fading red marks, they clearly weren't from a cat.

"Well, I hope you'll be happy working here," Annie said.

Sunny snuck a look at her watch. "Thanks, I've got to run. I still have a last shift in that pit." She giggled. "I'm really looking forward to handing in that resignation."

Annie and Alice watched her hurry away. "She really doesn't seem like a criminal mastermind type," Alice said quietly.

"Not really."

Linda waved them over to the front desk, and Annie stood quietly as Linda chatted with Alice about some of the things she'd seen in the catalog. Then Annie drifted over to the French doors that lead into the large dining room, the room that had been the ballroom during the party. The alcove where she'd been standing now held a single table, making a nice out-of-the-way nook.

Annie realized that standing in the nook would have made it easier for someone to find her and grab the hair comb. The person could use the wall line to avoid losing direction or running into anyone. That would mean someone standing near the wall already would have an easier time. Annie squinted, trying to picture the people she'd noticed after the theft. Which of them had stood close to the wall?

She was so deep in thought that she jumped and yelped when a hand came down on her shoulder.

"Sorry," Alice said. "I didn't mean to scare you. What are you doing?"

"Trying to remember who was standing where when the lights went out." Annie pointed toward the alcove. "The easiest way to reach me would have been to follow the wall line. If someone ran his hand along the wall, he could easily find the alcove. Then he could just grab the hair comb when I spoke and identified my position."

"That would work," Alice said, "but I don't really remember where people were standing. I was focused on us."

Annie sighed. "So was I. By the time I really looked around after the lights came on, people could have shifted positions quite a bit." She smiled a bit ruefully. "Seems none of our good ideas are really getting us any closer to solving this mystery."

Alice patted her friend on the arm. "We'll sort it out. For now, I think we're done here. You still need to go to the post office?"

Annie nodded, and they turned to walk out of the ballroom. From the lobby, they could see through the long windows that flanked the doubled front doors and showed the front porch. What they saw made them both stop.

John MacFarlane stood on the porch, smiling down at Sunny Day. The young woman leaned toward him with her hand on his arm. The overall effect was flirty and very intimate. "That jerk," Alice muttered.

They stepped back into the ballroom, not wanting to step out on the porch as long as they'd have to interact with John. "Well, that looked cozy," Alice said. "Maybe Sunny turned out the lights so John could grab your hair comb."

"I thought you'd eliminated him as a suspect," Annie said.

"That's before I saw him practically bobbing for apples in that young woman's neckline," Alice grumbled.

"I don't think it was quite that bad."

"Still, they looked pretty friendly," Alice said. "Why wouldn't John swipe something if he wanted to give a present to his new girlfriend."

"But what about Harry Stevens?" Annie asked. "Besides, Richard said he was sure it was a man on the cellar steps."

"He said it was dark," Alice reminded her. "Richard could have been wrong."

Annie looked at her friend skeptically. "Can you imagine any man running straight into Sunny Day and confusing her for a man?"

"OK, I give," Alice grumbled, holding up her hands in surrender.

They fell silent then as John passed by them, heading across the lobby. Alice stiffened as if she were considering going after him, but then her shoulders slumped and she said, "Let's go to the post office."

When they pulled into the parking lot at the post office, Alice turned to Annie, "If you don't mind, I'm going to wait in the car. I'm feeling grumpy enough without a chat with Norma."

"No problem."

Annie carried her project bag into the post office and peered at the spinning rack of padded envelopes and boxes, trying to decide which size she needed. She picked up a small box and held it up beside the bundle of fabric.

"An envelope ought to be plenty big enough," Norma said from behind the counter. "Unless you've got money to throw away."

"Do any of us have that?" Annie asked as she pulled out

a padded envelope and carried it to the counter. She pushed in the fabric and wrote LeeAnn's address on the outside before handing the package over to Norma.

The older woman took hold of the glasses that hung around her neck on a beaded chain and slipped them on. She peered at the address. "They don't have fabric shops in Texas?"

Annie smiled, and decided to try a little New England frugality. "Why buy fabric when I can give it to her? Saves money."

"Good thinking," Norma said approvingly. She laid the package on the scale as the door to the post office opened. Annie turned, wondering if Alice had gotten tired of waiting in the car. Instead she saw Mary Beth walk in.

"Hi," Annie said. "Did you see Alice outside?"

"I did and promised to rush you out," Mary Beth replied, smiling.

Norma cleared her throat, pulling attention back to her. She told Annie the price of the postage and Annie quickly paid, stepping aside so Mary Beth could step up and ask for some stamps.

"So, you and Alice are sleuthing today?" Mary Beth asked, risking the wrath of Norma by turning away from the counter while Norma rooted around for the special stamps Mary Beth wanted.

"Not very effectively," Annie said.

Norma cleared her throat again, pushing the stamps across the counter and collecting Mary Beth's money. "The diner's just down the road," Norma said gruffly. "It's a nice place to chat."

Annie almost laughed at Norma's grumpy hint that she didn't like chitchat in the post office. She caught sight of a mischievous sparkle in Mary Beth's eye. "I heard you saw the young woman from the ball," Mary Beth said, casually turning away from the counter.

"We did," Annie said, "but that was not the high point of the investigation for Alice."

The smile slipped from Mary Beth's face. "I know this has been tough for Alice. I'm glad to see she's showing some spirit though. Honestly, Annie, you wouldn't have known her when she first came home."

The post office door opened again and both women turned to look as Norma tried another throat clearing to move them along. Harry Stevens stepped through the door, carrying a small stack of packages. He took one look at Annie and Mary Beth, and then glanced back at the door as if considering a strategic retreat.

"May I help you?" Norma called.

"Um, yeah," Harry carried the boxes to the counter, stepping carefully around Annie and Mary Beth, but not speaking to them. "Got some stuff to mail for my father." He pushed the pile of packages onto the counter, and Norma began to weigh them.

Annie and Mary Beth moved back toward the door as Harry finished his business. When he finally turned to leave, Mary Beth said, "I heard Sunny Day was getting a job here in Stony Point. That'll be nice."

He looked at them in surprise. "At the diner?"

"No, at Maplehurst Inn."

He frowned slightly. "Linda hired her?"

"That is how someone gets a job at the inn," Mary Beth said drily.

Harry shrugged. "It's nothing to me. We just went to that party together. We're not *together*."

"Well, considering that girl is probably less than ten years older than your *daughter*, that's good," Mary Beth said.

Annie looked at her friend in surprise. In many ways, Mary Beth was practically the town mom. She was always so warm and welcoming, but she was going after Harry like a shark in a tuna tank.

Harry shifted uncomfortably. "Look, she dumped me, OK? Is that what you wanted to know? But it didn't have anything to do with my age! She wanted a guy with more money." Then he pushed past the two women and stormed out of the post office.

"You two sure add a ray of sunshine to this place," Norma said drily. "You want me to get you some chairs? You can wait for the next customer to run off."

Mary Beth turned to smile at Norma. "I'd take you up on that, but I need to get back to the shop. You'll just have to run people off on your own."

With that, she took Annie's arm and they left. Out on the sidewalk, Mary Beth started giggling, and soon she had Annie laughing too. Finally, Alice got out of her car to see what was so funny. Mary Beth admitted to giving Norma a hard time.

"I saw Harry Stevens storm out," Alice said, grinning. "Did you have anything to do with that as well?"

"Maybe a little," Mary Beth said. "You'll have to get Annie to catch you up though, I have to get back to the shop so Kate can go to lunch." She waved brightly as she hurried away.

Annie told Alice what they'd learned from Harry.

Alice snorted. "Well, that young woman is clearly misled if she thinks John is going to be her big spender."

"He does *look* like he has money. I can certainly see how Sunny Day would get that impression," Annie said as they walked back to Alice's car. The drive back to Grey Gables was quiet, with each woman lost in her own thoughts. Annie went over the mystery, though she suspected it was something much more personal that kept Alice so quiet.

Annie hopped out at Grey Gables and waved as Alice pulled around and headed back to her own driveway. The day had been full of revelations, but Annie wasn't sure if any of them actually helped solve the mystery.

They knew that someone was in the cellar at Maplehurst Inn and intentionally turned out the lights. That someone was probably the man who ran into Richard Bent on the steps. They knew that Harry and Sunny had not been a serious couple and that Sunny had not been scratched by a cat.

Annie had glanced at Harry's hands in the post office, but they were covered with the normal scratches and scrapes of a fisherman. She couldn't have said for sure that none might have been from Boots. But she also could see no reason why he would be playing games with the lights at the ball.

Annie stopped beside her burgundy Malibu and patted it absently as she thought about Sunny's apparent relationship with John MacFarlane. She supposed it was possible the two had known each other before, but neither showed signs of cat scratches. The whole idea felt too much like a conspiracy theory to her.

An odd sense of something being out of place drew Annie's attention to where her hand rested on the car. That's when she realized her passenger-side door was open a crack. Certainly she couldn't have driven the car with the door open, but she'd had no one in the car in over a week.

Annie pulled the door the rest of the way open and looked inside. She opened the glove box and saw her normal items, now in disarray. Someone had definitely been in her car! Since there was nothing of value in the car, she wasn't surprised to find nothing missing.

As Annie slid back out of the car, she struggled to remember clearly if she'd locked up after she used it last. She'd tried to get into the habit of locking up carefully after someone had broken into her car in the past, but she had to admit she didn't always remember, especially when her mind was on other things.

She turned nervous eyes toward Grey Gables. If someone had been in her car, were they in her house now? Annie reached into her project bag for her cell phone. Should she call Ian? Alice? Chief Edwards? Who did she least mind taking the risk of looking like a hysterical female in front of?

None. She dropped the phone back into her bag and marched up the steps. The front door was locked as she'd left it, and she gave a small sigh of relief. As she stepped inside, Boots trotted up to her and threaded through her legs.

"Well, looks like things are normal with *you*," she said. Since Boots had always reacted to strangers in the house, Annie felt a small measure of relief. Whoever had searched her car had not been in the house.

Still, that didn't change the fact that someone had searched her car. Someone wanted that small box of costume jewelry and apparently wasn't giving up on getting it. What Annie had to do was find out who—before the person got desperate.

— 17 —

Annie spent the rest of the day inside Grey Gables with the doors locked. She tried to tell herself that she wasn't doing it because she was afraid, but the reality was that she just couldn't face another unpleasant surprise. She wanted a quiet day wrapped in the warmth of Grey Gables and all her memories there.

"Just a little bit of hiding," she told Boots, who looked at her with mild interest. "Then tomorrow we have a Hook and Needle Club meeting. I'll get back in the swing of things then."

So Annie turned her attention to Gram's room. She still hadn't finished packing up Gram's personal things and moving them to the attic. She really didn't want Gram's room to become a shrine, though she'd keep a few things out.

"Not a shrine," she whispered. "Just a place that feels like family."

She decided to tackle the closet and go through Gram's scrap-fabric boxes to sort out some pieces she might want to use for Christmas presents. She'd seen a cute pattern at A Stitch in Time for baskets crocheted from rags. So the day passed in a cheerful haze of good memories and plans for the upcoming holidays.

The next morning brought a renewed sense of purpose. Annie was not going to be bullied; she was going to solve this mystery! After feeding her demanding, fluffy gray room-mate, she settled down at the kitchen table with coffee and her notepad where she'd been keeping track of what she'd uncovered so far.

She looked down her list of suspects. Harry Stevens and Sunny Day. Sunny had definitely not been scratched by a cat. Harry could have been. There was no way to pick out cat scratches in the day-to-day wear on a fisherman's hands. Sunny had shown an interest in Annie's jewelry, and Harry seemed genuinely sad that she'd dumped him. Would he have broken into her house to get something to give her, something to make him seem like a richer man than he was?

He'd broken into her car once before when he thought he had a good reason. He'd even started a rock slide that could have killed her. No, Harry Stevens was impulsive and stubborn when he felt like he had good cause. But would he really want Sunny that much?

She thought a moment about seeing Sunny with John. They certainly didn't look like strangers. What if John had put Sunny up to grabbing the hair comb, and Sunny used her obvious charms to send Harry to ransack Annie's house? She could certainly imagine John MacFarlane doing some-thing every bit that devious. But why would he want the jewelry? Unlike Sunny or Harry, John seemed likely to know the jewelry wasn't real once he got a close look at it.

Annie slipped the photo out of her pocket and looked again at the laughing woman in the emerald necklace. What if John knew something about this woman? Something about the scandal? Something someone would pay money to keep quiet. She could also imagine him involved in blackmail. But she had to admit, her personal feelings colored her impressions. At this point, she could imagine him guilty of nearly anything.

Boots broke her train of thought with a soft meow. She had finished her breakfast and was ready for a little attention. Annie reached down and stroked the cat's head. "You're probably right," she said. "I'm letting my imagination run away with me."

Annie put the notepad in her overflowing project bag and left for the meeting, crossing her fingers that Stella would be there. If Stella could just solve the mystery of who was in the photo, Annie was certain they'd finally begin to make sense of this.

Pulling into a parking space, she was surprised to see Stella standing in front of A Stitch in Time. The older woman was clearly in an intense conversation with Jenna Paige.

As Annie got out of her car and walked toward them, she could hear Stella's sharp tone. She was scolding Jenna about something. Just as Annie got close enough to make out actual words, Jenna turned away from Stella and ran across the street, heedless of the traffic. A driver had to slam on his brakes to avoid hitting the young woman, and he honked in annoyance. Jenna never even looked at him.

"What was that about?" Annie asked when she reached Stella.

Stella turned fiercely toward her. "I know you like your little mysteries, but that young woman is entirely too nosy! It's time she was told that strangers are not welcome to pry into the private lives of people here."

Annie blinked. "What did she do?"

"I'll not discuss it." Stella swept by her and into the shop. Annie followed meekly in her wake. She'd honestly all but given up on considering Jenna and Simon as suspects. She flatly couldn't picture the young woman being that secretive or sneaky.

As they walked in, the others were already there. Mary Beth looked up and smiled, "We're getting caught up on the mystery," she said.

"Mary Beth was just getting to the part where you two were tormenting Norma," Alice said.

Stella made a dismissive sound as she walked to her chair and sat down. "Norma may not be the most personable resident, but at least she never probes into the business of others."

Mary Beth looked at Stella in surprise. "Was that meant to be a rebuke for our mystery?"

"Take it however you want." Stella pulled out her knitting and then looked around the circle. No one else had a project out. "I seem to remember that we're a needlework group, right? Perhaps I'm the only one who remembers."

Peggy meekly pulled her bag into her lap and took out a place mat she was quilting, but everyone else just stared at Stella.

"I think Stella is a bit tired of interacting with Jenna Paige," Annie said hesitantly.

Stella looked up at her sharply. "I can speak for myself. I'm sure I've said that before."

"At least once," Alice said, her tone showing she wasn't the least bit cowed by Stella's aristocratic scorn.

"So what did Jenna do?" Mary Beth asked.

"I don't care to talk about it," Stella answered.

"We could guess," Alice said, her smile turning wicked. "She asked you how much money you have."

"Hardly," Stella said, her eyes never rising from her knitting.

"She asked if you were romantically involved with Jason?" Mary Beth suggested.

That brought a sharp glance from Stella. "Don't be ridiculous."

Gwen clearly couldn't resist joining in and she leaned forward and said in a loud whisper. "She asked you how old you are."

"I said I didn't want to discuss this!" Stella's tone rose so sharply that they all knew Gwen had hit the target.

"Well, honestly, I don't think Jenna's involved in the mystery anyway," Alice said. "There is something weird about her, but I don't see her as a jewel thief."

Gwen shrugged. "I'm not completely certain."

"Stella?" Annie said gently. "There is one more little thing you could do to help with the mystery."

Stella looked up. "I am not talking to that girl again."

Annie slipped the folded photo from her pocket. "No, I don't need you to do that. I was wondering if you might know who the woman is in this photo? It's from a newspaper, but I don't know which one or when it was published. The woman is wearing the emerald necklace from the set." Annie passed the paper over to Stella.

Stella stared at the photo for a long moment without speaking. "That's Millicent Winters. I haven't thought about her in years."

"Was she involved in some kind of scandal?"

"I would say so," Stella said, frowning slightly. "She killed her husband's mistress."

A collective gasp swept over the group.

"How much do you know about it?" Annie asked.

"What I read in the newspapers at the time," Stella said. "And what I heard. I didn't really know Millicent, but we were of a similar social status, and sometimes our social engagements overlapped. I believe she had a summer home here. I'd spoken to her a few times. She was an astoundingly proud woman. Almost arrogant."

"Did she go to prison for the murder?" Alice asked.

Stella looked up, and again her brows drew together in a frown as she thought. "I don't remember. I know there was a tremendous outcry from the public, and the police were under a lot of pressure to arrest her. It wasn't easy to arrest the very wealthy in those days."

"Why would the police hesitate?" Kate asked.

"They couldn't find the young woman's body," Stella said. "She simply disappeared. I believe they did find blood at the scene but only a tiny bit. No body, no arrest. Certainly not with such a wealthy suspect."

"So what happened to Millicent Winters?" Annie asked.

"I don't know," Stella said. "She stopped attending social functions. They may have moved. Or the police may have arrested her. I truly don't remember. I just know I never personally saw her again after the scandal made the news."

"OK, so Millicent Winters once owned the jewelry, and she might have killed someone," Alice said. "That doesn't really help us know who is trying to get the jewelry. We certainly don't have any suspects who are that age."

"No," Annie said. "But what if this jewelry is connected somehow to the murder? What if someone wants to use them to blackmail someone or to cover up something?"

"Are you sure you're not being a little overly imaginative?" Stella asked.

"No," Annie answered. "I'm not sure. Maybe I am. But I'm thinking I really need to get to the bottom of this. My house was broken into on the night of the ball. My car was searched the day before yesterday."

That brought another gasp, and Alice demanded to know why Annie hadn't told her.

"Nothing was taken," Annie said. "And it was done while I was away. I didn't know what good it would do to tell anyone."

"So what do you think we should do next?" Peggy asked, glancing at Stella nervously from the corner of her eye. Of all the members of the Hook and Needle Club, Peggy hated it most when Stella disapproved of their actions. She idolized the older woman.

"I do have an idea," Annie said. "Or the bones of one. I think we need to push the thief into doing something. I believe we need to spread a rumor of our own."

"What kind?" Alice said.

"What if we let everyone know that I'm taking the jewelry to sell to Milt Koenig on Thursday?" Annie said. "And then I make a big show of going out somewhere with all of you for dinner or something tomorrow. That would make the perfect time for a break-in. And if we double back, we can catch the housebreaker in the act."

"It's tricky and sneaky," Alice said. "I like it."

Mary Beth looked concerned. "It sounds dangerous."

"How about if I promise to tell Ian and Chief Edwards?" Annie asked. "Would you feel better then?"

Mary Beth nodded. "All right—if you do that, I'm in. How do we make sure all our suspects get the word?"

"I can tell Vanessa and make sure she slips it to her father tonight," Kate said. "He's supposed to be going to her chorus concert."

"I can have Ian pass it on to Todd," Annie said. "And Todd could tell Jenna and Simon. From what Ian said, they spend a lot of time on his boat."

"When they aren't bothering people in the street," Stella muttered.

"I need to call Victoria Meyer about her favorite charity," Gwen said. "The bank is planning to make a donation. At any rate, I can slip it into the conversation. If you still consider her a suspect."

Annie sighed. "She's the only suspect in the same social standing as the original owner. And she definitely wants the jewelry, although hearing the rumor will probably just encourage her to try to buy it again."

"I'll work it into as many conversations at the diner as I can," Peggy said.

"Oh, you should tell people where in the house you're going to keep the jewels," Alice said. "That way you won't end up having to clean the place up again."

"I'm hoping to catch the person *before* much mess is made," Annie said. "Still, how about the freezer? I had a neighbor once who hid money in the freezer. It always seemed like a funny place."

"The freezer," Peggy said. "Got it!"

Annie knew there were few ways to get the word out better than Peggy's diner hotline. Then she made a mental note to mention it in front of Ian's secretary. Charlotte could be busy in the Stony Point gossip network too.

"So where are we all going together?" Gwen asked. "And do we actually get to go? We could go to the History of Dance performance at the Cultural Center. I've been meaning to get tickets to that. Liz Booth told me the community dance ensemble did a wonderful job with the choreography, and they're performing it for the next three nights."

"Oh, now you make me wish I was going with you," Annie said. "So, will that be our cover story?"

"I would be willing to go to that as well," Stella said.

"I'm afraid you'll have to count me out," Peggy said sadly, then she added. "One major social event is all I can fit into my social season."

"I'll have to skip as well," Kate said. "But we don't all have to go. We just have to make it look like Annie's house is going to be empty."

"So we all have the rumor down?" Annie asked. Each person repeated what they would be spreading around. As Annie listened to them coordinate her story, she hoped this would turn out to be a good idea. A lot of those television mystery shows featured plans that went spectacularly wrong. She hoped that wouldn't be the case with hers.

After the meeting, Annie headed across the Town Square toward Town Hall. The grass of the square was nearly covered by the fallen leaves from the maples and oaks that lined the Oak Lane and Elm Street sides of the square.

Annie even indulged in kicking the crispy leaves into the air as she walked. She'd loved doing that when she was a child, walking home from school and kicking the autumn leaves with each step.

When she reached the wide Town Hall steps, she brushed the leaves off her shoes and pant legs.

"Too late," a male voice said from above her. "I saw you."

Annie looked up and smiled at Ian Butler. "I couldn't resist. They were so perfectly crispy."

Ian laughed. "Don't tell anyone, but I've done it too. Were you on your way to see me?"

"I was," Annie said as she walked up the steps to join him at the top. "I want to talk to you about a plan to unmask my housebreaker."

Ian frowned slightly. "Why am I not liking this already?"

"Would you like it better if I didn't tell you about it?"

"No." He folded his arms across his chest. "You should tell me everything."

"That could take a while."

He pulled open the door. "Then we should continue this in my office."

Annie followed him down the warm, well-polished wood floors of Town Hall. She noticed Charlotte staring at her sharply as they walked by the older woman's desk. Charlotte clearly had not yet decided if she was happy with *her* mayor spending so much time with Annie Dawson.

Ian closed the office door behind them and gestured to the well-padded leather chair that faced his desk. He took the other visitor chair beside hers. "All right," he said.

"Catch me up on the Annie Dawson mystery."

Annie told him about visiting Maplehurst Inn, and what they'd learned from the handyman. Ian shifted anxiously as she spoke. "I'd hoped that blackout was an accident or power overload," he said, "but it sounds like someone deliberately turned off the power."

"But we're not certain they did it to take my hair comb," Annie said. "It could have been a practical joke, or someone wanting to make Linda Hunter's life difficult. It did result in complaints. The blackout could have simply been coincidental and convenient for the thief."

Ian nodded. "I've talked to Chief Edwards. The theft of your jewelry and the break-in at your house were the only odd things reported that evening."

"Which suggests that someone wants those pieces very badly," Annie said. "And that's backed up by the break-in of my car."

"What?" Ian leaned forward, face serious.

"Nothing was taken," Annie said. "And I wasn't home. I was with Alice doing sleuthing at the inn. While we were there, we spotted John MacFarlane looking very friendly with Harry's date from the ball."

Ian winced. "How did Alice handle that?"

"She didn't confront him," Annie said, "but we can definitely be sure she's not going to let him snow her under with anything."

"Well, that's good," Ian said. He paused, deep in thought. "If this friendship between Sunny and John is long-standing, they may have been using Harry on the night of the ball."

"I've talked to Sunny several times, and she doesn't

seem the mastermind type," Annie said. "But I'm not sure about John."

Annie went on to tell Ian what Stella had told her about the photo.

"I don't remember anything about that," Ian said. "It was before my time."

Finally, Annie shared the plan the Hook and Needle Club members had cooked up. "Whoever wants these jewels isn't going to want me to sell them," she said. "A jewelry store is definitely harder to break into than an old house. I figured this is going to force the housebreaker to act. Alice and I will pretend to go out with Stella and Gwen tomorrow night. Then we'll double back and wait. I was thinking you might want to wait with us?"

"I certainly don't want you to wait alone," Ian said. "But I'm not in love with this plan. What if this person is desperate? You could get hurt."

"That's why we're letting you join our group," Annie said.

"Well, you sound determined, and I know better than to try to talk you out of it," he said. "I'll be there. How do you suggest we go about this?"

"You could hide out at Alice's," Annie said. "Then we could all sneak back through Alice's backyard. There's an overgrown strip of brush back there that connects to my yard. Then we'll just sneak in the back door and wait."

Ian still did not look convinced, but he nodded. "OK, we'll do this. But I'm telling Chief Edwards just in case we need him."

Annie nodded. "There's one more thing. I was hoping

we could talk about the plan to sell the jewels, and my plan to go to the dance performance in front of Charlotte." Her face warmed slightly as she spoke. She didn't like to criticize people, but she knew Charlotte would definitely help get the word out about their "plans."

Ian leaned back in his chair and smiled slightly. "That shouldn't be too hard," he said. "Charlotte's not going to be able to stand us being alone in here too much longer. We can wait until she comes in with some reason for interrupting and just be sure to go over your cover story while she's here."

"Sounds like you know your secretary well," Annie said.

"Well enough."

Just then, there was a light knock and the door to Ian's office opened, and Charlotte hurried in with a small pile of papers. "I'm sorry to interrupt, Mr. Mayor," she said primly, "but you didn't sign these forms yet for the budget meeting."

Ian smiled. "Of course." Then he turned to Annie as he held his hands out for the papers. "I think it's a good idea for you to do something fun for a change. I've heard good things about that dance performance. When are you going?"

"We're riding with Stella," Annie said, noticing Charlotte's eagle eyes turning sharply to her as she spoke. "She's picking us up tomorrow evening around seven."

"I hope you have a good time," he said, his head down to glance over the papers. "But don't stay out too late if you're driving to Storm Harbor on Thursday."

"Well, that's when Milt Koenig said he'd like to meet," she said. "I'll be glad to have that jewelry off my hands. They've caused me nothing but headaches. And they belong back with his family since his grandfather made the pieces."

Ian held the pen over the paper, but looked up suddenly at Annie. "Would you like me to put the jewelry in my safe until then?"

"No, they're fine. I'm keeping them in the freezer. I just wrapped the whole box in aluminum foil. I saw that on a television show."

"I saw that show," Charlotte said. "I thought that was a great idea, but I haven't tried it yet."

Ian scrawled his signature and handed the papers back to Charlotte. "Thank you, Charlotte."

"Will you be leaving for lunch soon?" she asked Ian.

He turned to look at Annie. "Good idea. Want to join me for lunch?"

Annie smiled. "Maybe a quick one. Then I have to pick up some groceries at Magruder's."

As Annie followed Ian out the door of his office, she noticed Charlotte scurrying back to her desk. Something told Annie it wouldn't be long before Charlotte thought of someone who would like to hear a bit of gossip. She just hoped her plan wasn't lost in Charlotte ranting about the mayor spending too much time with a certain widow.

Lunch was pleasant, and Annie thought again about how much nicer it was to eat in the well-lit diner than at that dreadful place in Storm Harbor. Peggy slipped over to their table once to whisper, "I'm spreading the word."

Between Peggy and Charlotte, Annie was sure everyone in Stony Point would know that Grey Gables would be empty on Wednesday night.

~ 18 ~

After lunch, Annie crossed the street and walked down to Magruder's Groceries. As she drifted through the aisles, plucking something off the shelf whenever it caught her eye, she thought again of her grandmother. Betsy Holden never shopped without a list, but sometimes Annie liked to be inspired by what she saw. Her husband used to tease her about "inspiration shopping," but he always seemed to enjoy the meal variety that it produced.

As she picked up a small tin of English tea, she shook her head ruefully. It was hard to believe that inspiration shopping used to be about the most adventurous thing in her life. She'd liked the steadiness of her life in Texas. There was something comforting in the familiarity of each day, but even though her life in Stony Point could be a little too exciting sometimes, she found it went a long way toward waking her up from the fog of loss she'd been in when she'd first returned.

"Mrs. Dawson?"

Annie turned to face Jenna Paige. The young woman held a shopping basket and looked at Annie anxiously. "Yes?" Annie said. "Are you all right?"

Jenna nodded, but then her eyes filled with tears, and she shook her head. "I don't know."

"What's the matter?" Annie asked.

"Do you like me?" Jenna asked quietly.

"I hardly know you," Annie replied gently, "but you seem like a very friendly person."

"I try to be," Jenna said. "And I hoped people here would like me, but I don't think they do." She wrapped an arm around herself, as if she were cold.

"Why would it matter? You will be done with your research soon, won't you?"

Jenna nodded, then she stepped closer to Annie. "Can I tell you a secret?"

"If you want."

"Simon and I are getting married," she said softly. "And we thought we might like to live here. It's such a pretty town, and it's close to the water. I love the water. I even thought I might teach. Simon was offered a position at the University of Maine, and I thought I might ... "

Annie looked at her quizzically.

"Don't laugh," Jenna said.

"I won't," Annie promised.

"I thought I might write a children's book," Jenna said. "About ocean life and what we can do to protect it. I even know who the main character will be—Lolly the Lobster." She sighed. "Anyway, it seemed like a wonderful idea, but some of the people here can really be so *mean*."

Annie felt of pang of guilt as she looked at the tearful young woman, since she was certain Stella's scolding must have upset her terribly. Stella wouldn't have let her temper build up so much if she wasn't trying to solve Annie's mystery. As far as Annie was concerned, that laid the blame squarely at Annie's door.

"I'm sorry Stella was short with you," she said. "I'll tell you a secret. She didn't like me very much when I first moved here. She thought I was nosy."

Jenna's eyes opened wide. "She did? Did she say that?"

"More than once," Annie said, "though maybe not as forcefully as she told you. But really, she's just not comfortable with new people. Once she gets used to you, it will be different."

Jenna looked thoughtful for a moment, and then she shook her head. "She's not the only one. Some people just glared at us when we went to the ball."

At least Annie knew that wasn't related to her over-zealous mystery hunters. "Well," she said gently, "lobster fishing is very important around here. I think having researchers here to count lobsters and such makes people afraid that new regulations could appear that would make it harder to make a living."

"Really?" she said with a sniff. "You think that's it?"

"Could be."

"So they don't just … not like me?"

Annie patted the girl's arm. "I don't know why anyone wouldn't like you." Then she paused before she continued. "May I offer you some advice?"

Jenna nodded eagerly, looking a bit more like herself.

"When I first moved here," Annie said. "It took a long time for me to feel like I was fitting in. Stella wasn't the only person who wasn't exactly nice to me then, and I felt terrible about it."

"What did you do?" Jenna asked.

"I tried to give them space, and maybe not be quite so

eager," Annie said. "I tried to be patient. And you know? Some of the people who were coldest to me are among my best friends now, and we're all in that needlework group you met at Mary Beth's shop."

A smile brightened Jenna's face. "They're very nice. I don't think I'd join a needlework group, though. I finally gave up on that cross-stitch when Simon told me the back side of the cloth looked like it had a fuzzy animal stuck to it."

"May I ask you something?" Annie said, remembering that Simon had scratches that could be from Boots. "It might seem like a strange one."

"Sure, anything," Jenna said.

"Is Simon's family from around here?"

Jenna smiled and shook her head. "No, Simon's from Louisiana. That's where all his family lives. Simon's the first member of the family to ever get an advanced degree. They're very proud of him, and they're all really nice people—" she giggled a little, "—even if I can't always understand everything they say. Have you ever been to Louisiana? The accent is amazing." She leaned closer to Annie again for another whisper. "That's the other place we're considering moving to. Simon got an offer down there too."

Annie admitted she'd never been there. As Jenna continued to spill out all kinds of details of different relatives and exciting things about Louisiana, Annie decided they really could safely mark another suspect off the list. It didn't seem like Simon or Jenna could be connected with the scandal or the jewelry. Still, just to be sure, Annie worked in a remark about selling the jewelry on Thursday.

"Oh, you mean that pretty hair comb you wore to the

ball?" Jenna asked. "That was beautiful. I don't think you should sell it. It looked really nice on you."

"Thank you," Annie said, "but I lost the comb at the ball. I'm just going to sell the rest of the pieces. The grandson of the man who designed them would like to have them. I'm going to sell them on Thursday."

"Oh, that would be nice," Jenna said. "I always wished I came from a close family." This launched another gush of information about how many children Jenna hoped to have, and her hopes they'd all be very close. Annie let the girl's chatter pour over her for a bit, and then she asked her if she knew about the dance performance at the Cultural Center.

"No, is it ballet?" Jenna asked. "I've always thought I'd like to see a ballet."

"I think it's historical somehow," Annie said. "A bunch of us are planning to go Wednesday night. It'll be good to get out of the house."

Jenna giggled. "I'm looking forward to having a nice house to get out of someday."

Eventually, even Jenna ran out of things to talk about, and Annie was able to ease away. She paid for her groceries and headed home, feeling a little like she could use a nap after the deluge of chatter from the young scientist.

Afternoon shadows were slanting across the lawn as Annie pulled up in front of Grey Gables. Annie scooped up her two cloth grocery bags and carried them to the house, managing to hook a last finger through one handle on her project bag.

The groceries seemed to get heavier with each step, and she suddenly wished she'd made two trips. *That's the trouble with impulse shopping*, she thought. *Your impulses can get really heavy!* When she got to the porch, she tried to shift the load so she could set one of the heavy bags down in the seat of the nearest white wicker porch chair.

As she struggled with the groceries, her project bag slipped off her finger, spilling its contents before hitting the porch. "That's what I get for being in a hurry," she moaned, looking at the mess. She lugged her bags into the kitchen before returning to the porch.

She bent down and began scooping balls of yarn and hooks into the bag. She saw that the flat wooden jewelry box had sprung open and the velvet-covered form where the jewelry nestled had fallen out, along with the brooch and necklace.

She picked up the brooch, and then spent a moment picking the necklace out of the crack in the porch planks where it had fallen. She tilted the box back right-side up. That's when she saw the folded paper wedged under the molded velvet box lining.

She picked out the folded sheet, stuck it in her pocket, and placed the liner and jewelry back in the box. The mysterious paper seemed to call out to her from her pocket; she sank into one of the living-room chairs and opened the paper. It was a note.

Dear Betsy,

I know we don't know each other well. I've not always returned your friendly kindness in a way that reflects well on me. I'm sorry for that. But when I think of people I can trust with a secret, your name is the only one that comes to mind.

I should dispose of this jewelry, but somehow I cannot.

When my husband gave me these for our anniversary last year, I still believed in him. I remember the joy I felt, and how I looked forward to our future. I can't simply throw that away, even if I can't stand to look at them, knowing he'd taken them and handed them over to that cheap woman.

I assure you, these are evidence of no crime. What the newspapers are saying is not true. I never hurt that strumpet beyond ripping my personal belongings from her ears. And I certainly gave her enough money to make up for any discomfort. I paid for a new name and for her to relocate to a new country. She deserved neither. I only took what was rightfully mine. I refuse to see that as a crime!

I must live with the shame of buying my husband back from a diner waitress, but I will not have the world knowing. I firmly believe this scandal will blow over since I am not guilty, but at least my real secret can remain mine. I guess that says something about my pride. I would rather be thought a murderess than a weakling.

Someday, I may want these back. I don't know. But I can't have them near me. Not now. I must focus on my family. Nothing else matters. You now have my jewelry—and my most hideous secret—in your hands. I trust you to keep them safe.

Annie stared at the letter in amazement. It was signed with initials only: M.W. Annie knew they must stand for Millicent Winters. As she stared at the paper, Annie shook her head sadly. What a terrible price this woman must have paid for the sake of pride.

With shaking hands, Annie slipped the paper back into her pocket. Was someone willing to steal to keep this secret from the past? If so, who was doing it? Who wanted to keep Millicent Winters's story buried?

With a sigh, Annie decided to fire up her laptop and see if she could find anything about the murder or about Millicent Winters. She carried the laptop to the kitchen again. If she was going to tackle the search on her own, she preferred to do it in the room she felt most comfortable in.

Annie tapped her fingers on the worn wooden table as she waited for her computer to boot up. Millicent Winters was desperate to keep a secret that was tied to the jewelry. But she would have to be an old woman today. So who was still interested in this secret?

Annie clicked on her Internet icon, and then waited for her homepage to load. She used a search engine for her homepage since she figured the only time she would consider turning on the computer, she'd have to be desperate to know something.

She typed "Millicent Winters" into the search box and clicked the button to start the search. She quickly learned there was a town named Millicent that booked tourists in the winter. She discovered a couple of profiles for women named "Millicent Winters," but they were all quite young. Then she found a link to "Unsolved Mysteries of the Past."

That sounded promising. Annie clicked on it and soon was looking at a Web page that featured graphics made to look like wanted posters. She scanned the links and found the one labeled "Death of a Diner Waitress." The brief write-up covered mostly just what Annie already knew with the addition of a few names.

A young waitress named Tracey Williams had vanished.

The police found trace amounts of her blood on the carpet in her apartment but not enough to suggest the woman was killed there.

During the investigation, they discovered the waitress had a wealthy lover, Jackson Winters. And a witness claimed the lover's wife had been at the waitress's apartment on the last night anyone had seen the girl. The write-up did mention that the witness only saw Mrs. Winters because he was sitting in the alley beside the apartment building, drinking.

There was no follow-up on the case and no resolution. The police only had one suspect, but they never had a body, so eventually the investigation simply stalled. Annie returned to the search engine and clicked through more links, but nothing else turned up even distantly related to the case. As she shut down the computer, Annie wondered if she should visit the library. There might be more information, maybe even newspaper reports.

Annie yawned and noticed that night had fallen while she'd read through the links. She decided to spend some time working on her sweater and unwind before bed. Tomorrow she might see the end of this mystery at last. As Annie glanced at the note on the table beside her, she wondered if this mystery could possibly have a happy ending for anyone.

Annie slept unusually late the next morning after having had some trouble falling asleep the night before. She might have stayed in bed even longer if Boots hadn't pushed her nose into Annie's and meowed. The sound and ticklish whiskers woke Annie at once, and she gently pushed the chubby cat toward the edge of the bed.

"OK, Miss Boots," she said. "I get it. Breakfast is unacceptably late."

Despite the cat's complaints, Annie decided to shower and dress before heading to the kitchen. By the time she gave in, Boots was nearly yowling with complaints about the slow service.

"Goodness," Annie said as she poured the dry food in the small ceramic cat dish. "You'd think you were an alley cat teetering on the brink of starvation."

Boots shoved her head into the bowl, not even bothering to go through her usual routine of scornful sniffing. As Annie carried the box of cat food back to the cupboard, she realized she hadn't yet put the "bait" in the freezer. She'd need to wrap something in foil—something that clearly would look like a jewelry box.

Annie scouted around for possible boxes in the cupboard but didn't find anything the right size. Then she peered into the freezer and pulled out a small box of vegetables and wrapped it in foil before sticking it back in. "Close enough," she said.

She wondered if she should make a run to the library. With the word out about the jewelry, it might be better if she didn't leave the house until the appointed moment. That way she wouldn't be inviting an early break-in with no one there to do the actual capturing of the crook!

That left her with a lot of hours and nothing really to do with them. She reread the note from Millicent Winters, knowing it was ridiculous to expect it to suddenly reveal fresh clues. Annie refolded the note and put it back in the jewelry box. "I really should have made a plan for what to do before the plan goes into motion," Annie said to Boots. The cat didn't even look up.

Annie carried her coffee out to the front room and curled up in the corner of the sofa to crochet. It might not keep her mind busy, but doing something with her hands would help her avoid pacing all day.

She'd finished one of the tricky sweater sleeves when her cell phone rang. She dug it out from under the pile of yarn in her bag and answered it just before it could roll over into voice mail.

"Did you know your phone is off the hook?" Alice's voice said as soon as Annie said hello.

"No," Annie stood and walked over to the table where the phone rested. She found the phone scooted to the edge of the table and the receiver halfway off the hook. For an instant Annie felt a jolt of alarm until she saw the fluffy gray hair caught under the edge of the phone.

"I guess Boots was making phone calls," Annie told Alice. "It's on now."

"You had me a little worried when you didn't answer," Alice said. "I'm glad I didn't panic and call in the cavalry."

Annie laughed. "And who would the cavalry constitute?"

"Ian. Can't you see him charging in on a white horse?"

"I really don't want to get in the habit of calling Ian every time I have a problem," Annie said.

"He's coming this evening though?"

"Yes," Annie said. "Besides, asking him gave me the perfect chance to mention our cover story in front of Charlotte. I didn't want to miss an opportunity to spread the word."

"You know, I'm kind of sorry we're missing the dance

performance. I hadn't paid much attention to it, but now that we're *not* going ... I wish I were."

"Well, if this mystery is solved tonight," Annie said, "we can go to one of the other performances."

"Good," Alice answered. "That's something to look forward to."

Then Annie told Alice about the note she'd found and how little she'd been able to learn about the case against Millicent Winters online. "If I weren't concerned about leaving the house too early, I'd go look it up at the library," Annie said.

"Is that a hint?"

"No, but if you wanted to go ..."

"No problem," Alice said laughing. "I owe you at least one research trip anyway for the help you gave Jim with his lighthouse mystery. And it'll help pass the time."

"Great, now I just have to find a way to pass the time myself." Annie glanced down at her watch. "Oh—I guess I'll start with lunch. It's later than I thought."

As soon as she hung up the phone, Annie heard the front doorbell. She opened the door and blinked in surprise when she saw Victoria Meyer standing on the front porch. "Good afternoon, Mrs. Dawson," the cool blonde said.

"Good afternoon. Would you like to come in?"

"If you don't mind."

Annie stepped away from the door, and the taller woman walked in, her eyes sweeping around the entry as if making a mental note of everything she saw. Victoria turned back to look at Annie. "I had hoped we might talk a bit."

"Of course. Would you like a cup of tea?"

"Yes, thank you."

Annie led Mrs. Meyer to the kitchen, constantly conscious of the tap of the taller woman's sharp heels on the wood floor behind her. Annie gestured toward the kitchen table where the afternoon sun flowing through the window made the old wood glow.

"This is a charming little house," Mrs. Meyer said.

"Thank you," Annie said as she put the kettle on the stove and reached into the cupboard, looking for two cups that matched. "It belonged to my grandmother. I inherited it from her."

"So I've been told. I understand you've found all sorts of things in the attic since you moved in."

"I am beginning to suspect Gram never threw anything away," Annie admitted.

"And apparently people entrusted her with things sometimes."

"Sometimes."

An awkward silence fell on the room, and the tension lay so thick in the air that Annie actually jumped when the kettle whistled. She poured the hot water over two tea bags and carried them to the table before slipping into the chair across from the young woman.

"I believe you've found more of the jewelry in the emerald set," Mrs. Meyer said. "Although I don't ordinarily indulge in gossip, I did hear you were going to sell some Milton Koenig jewelry to his grandson?"

"Why are you so interested in a set of costume jewelry?"

"I like the design," she said. "And since the designer has passed away, I can hardly get him to create something similar for me."

"But you could find any number of designers who could create jewelry for you."

She nodded. "But I am interested in this particular set."

"Why?"

"I don't see that as any of your concern," Mrs. Meyer said. "I have heard that you see yourself as some kind of amateur detective, Mrs. Dawson. But I see no need for you to detect your way into my personal business. I only wish to buy the remaining pieces of the set."

"Since you already have the earrings," Annie said. "And the hair comb."

The other woman narrowed her eyes as she looked at her. "I have the earrings, that's true. Are you saying there is a hair comb?"

"This is news to you?"

"Why wouldn't it be?"

"I wore the hair comb to the Harvest Ball," Annie said. "When the lights went out, someone pulled it out of my hair. Then my house was broken into."

Mrs. Meyer raised her eyebrows, then smiled coldly. "And you think I crept around in a dark ballroom, groped my way to wherever you were, and snatched a piece of costume jewelry from your hair?" She laughed without humor. "You do have as vivid an imagination as I have heard."

"I have nothing to sell to you," Annie said.

"I'm willing to pay handsomely."

"I don't need money."

Again the perfectly shaped brows rose and the cold gaze swept over the cozy kitchen. "Really?"

"My husband left me well provided for," Annie said.

"I'm really quite comfortable."

The two women stared at one another for another long, silent moment. The silence was interrupted when Boots stalked into the room and sat in the middle of the kitchen floor. She wrapped her tail regally around her and stared coldly at the stranger.

"Ah, this must be the demon cat my assistant told me about," Mrs. Meyer said. "I expected it to be bigger with alarming fangs."

"She can be surprisingly formidable," Annie said.

"So can I."

"I don't doubt that for a moment," Annie said. "You know, I'm getting a bit tired of people making ominous statements to me. I told you I have no jewelry to sell to you. Any examples of Milton Koenig's art I have in my possession will be sold to his grandson. I promised to do so, and that's what I intend to do."

"And what will he do with them?"

"He wants them as examples of his grandfather's skill," Annie said. "I wouldn't be surprised if he displays them in the shop. But it's difficult to say. Perhaps he would sell them to you if you offer enough money."

"That would be unacceptable."

Annie leaned forward. "Why?"

When the woman across the table didn't answer, Annie slipped her hand into her cardigan pocket and drew out the folded photo of the woman in the necklace that she still carried. She slid it across the table. "Who was this woman to you?"

"Where did you get this?" Mrs. Meyer whispered.

"Milt Koenig gave it to me. It's a copy of an old newspaper photo that his father had clipped because it showed one of Milton Koenig's designs," Annie said. "I know this is Millicent Winters, but who is she to you?"

The young woman gazed at the photo and ran her finger lightly over the curve of the laughing woman's cheek. "She was my mother."

Annie sat back, startled. "You don't look old enough to be this woman's child."

"I was a late-in-life baby, born after my parents finally separated. Mother had lost a baby quite a few years earlier. I always thought it was from the stress of the scandal. I assume you know all about the scandal?" She asked the question without emotion, and when Annie only nodded, she turned her eyes back to the photo. Finally, she tapped a perfectly tapered nail against the photo. "I never once saw her laugh like that."

"Because of the scandal."

"I'm not sure. Maybe. Or maybe it was the guilt of being a murderess."

Annie blinked in surprise. "She was not a killer."

"*What*?" The faint haze that had clouded the woman's eyes from the moment Annie unfolded the picture seemed to clear. The eyes that turned toward Annie then were razor sharp. "What are you talking about?"

"She didn't kill that waitress."

"How do you know?"

Annie got up and walked to the front room. She slipped the jewelry box from her project bag and carried it back into the kitchen. She set it before the young woman. "There's a note in there from your mother. I didn't see it at first—it was under the bottom lining. I only found it yesterday."

Victoria Meyer opened the box and lifted out the note. She held it with trembling fingers. Annie waited in the perfect silence of the kitchen. Finally, the young woman folded the note closed again and looked at Annie. "I never knew."

"You believed your mother had killed that waitress?"

"My father believed it, though we never talked about my mother. There really were so few times that he remembered I was his daughter, and that he ought to spend time with me." She looked back down into the jewelry case, touching the imitation gems gently. "My mother had Alzheimer's. I remember only a scant few days spent with her when her mind was clear, and we certainly didn't spend them talking about this scandal. On her bad days, she sometimes talked about the waitress, and about her shame and regret. I thought she was talking about the murder."

She looked back up at Annie. "I was terrified that seeing these gems would trigger someone's memory of those horrible times. I thought that the whole scandal would stir again, and that the whispers would begin again. I couldn't let that happen. I didn't want the scandal to destroy my marriage the way it did my mother's. My husband knows nothing about it." Then her voice dropped to little more than a whisper. "And I didn't want my child to grow up under that shadow."

"Your child?"

She nodded. "I'm not very far along yet. Not enough to show." Her eyes grew damp and she blinked away tears. "I've been so worried that all this would begin again, and she'd grow up the way I did."

"So you bought the mask I made and stole my hair comb when the lights went out."

She nodded.

"And you sent someone over to find the rest of the set?" Annie said.

She nodded again. "My assistant. The cat scratched his hands and arms up while he was searching. I think it's given him a phobia of cats." She looked back down at the jewelry. "May I have them? I'll pay you."

Annie smiled and laid a gentle hand on the young woman's arm. "You don't have to pay for them. They belong to you. My grandmother was only keeping them safe until someone wanted them back—someone to whom they rightfully belonged. You're that someone. You should take them with you."

"I'm sorry for what I did. I just ... I didn't think I had a choice. I loved my mother, even though the disease barely gave me any chance to know her."

"Not long ago," Annie said, "I didn't think I'd known my mother very well either. Not when she was alive. But sometimes you can get a second chance to learn. I got mine and maybe this is yours. Your mother was a proud woman, but she wasn't a killer."

Victoria Meyer smiled in wonder. "No, she was no killer."

The young woman finished her tea and slowly relaxed. She began to share the few nicer memories she had of her mother. Annie could almost see the weight lift off her shoulders as she spoke.

Victoria stood, slipping the small jewelry box into her handbag. "Thank you for everything," she said quietly. She looked toward the darkened kitchen window. "I should go. I heard you were going to the dance performance this evening, and I've kept you too long."

Annie's eyes grew wide, and she looked down at her watch. She'd completely forgotten about the plan, and her friends were due at any minute. "Oh, I have to make some phone calls," she said, edging toward the door. "But I'm glad we had this time together."

Victoria nodded. She followed Annie to the front door, and then she impulsively reached out and hugged Annie. "Thank you again," she said. "I feel like you gave me back my mother."

"You know," Annie said, "I didn't think this mystery could have a happy ending. It looks like I was wrong. I'm so glad."

Annie stood on the porch while Victoria walked out to her pale silver Lexus that shone in the light of the full moon. As the Lexus drove out onto the street, Stella's Lincoln Continental pulled in. Annie spotted Jason in the driver's seat and returned his nod.

As Gwen and Stella piled out of the car, Alice strode across the yard from the carriage house. "I'm so sorry," Annie called out. "The plan is off."

The three woman stopped and stared at her in surprise. "Why?"

"The mystery is solved. Do you want to come in and hear how it ended? I don't want you to miss your performance," she said.

"Forget the performance," Stella said. "Of course we

want to hear."

"Just let me go get Ian," Alice called, holding up a hand as she turned to trot back toward the carriage house. "Don't spill any secrets without me!"

Soon the whole group was gathered in the cheery parlor, sipping coffee and nibbling shortbread cookies while Annie told them all about Victoria's visit.

"My goodness," Stella said. "I would never have imagined that ending. Imagine keeping a secret like that."

"She told Gram," Annie said. "And I believe she would have told her daughter if the disease hadn't prevented it. I can't imagine she would have wanted Victoria to suffer. Family clearly mattered to her."

"Family and pride," Gwen said. "I've been guilty of that myself."

"And me," Stella admitted.

"Well, it sounds to me like Annie Dawson has done another good deed for Stony Point," Ian said, smiling at her warmly.

Annie felt her face flush slightly, and quickly she changed the subject. "You know what this means."

The group looked at her quizzically.

"It means Jenna Paige is just an over-eager, young woman who wanted to find a nice town," Annie said.

Stella sighed heavily. "I suppose I do owe her an apology."

"You don't think she's going to want to join the Hook and Needle Club?" Gwen asked anxiously.

"No, I think she's given up needlework. I don't even know if they will be moving here. She didn't sound sure, but if she finds out how friendly this town can be, I think we could be proud of that."

Stella grumbled a bit more, and Jason shot Annie a grin that showed he completely approved. Annie suspected Stella's driver and longtime friend could also be her conscience now and then.

"OK," Alice said, "I have something to tell about this mystery too. Something I found out today."

"At the library?"

"Not exactly," she said. "I ran into Linda Hunter on the street, and she told me John MacFarlane checked out of Maplehurst Inn and left town. I guess he didn't feel the need to say goodbye."

"How do you feel about that?" Annie asked.

"Mostly relieved," Alice said. "I'm finally feeling like that's a part of my life I can close the door on." Then she grinned. "I did hear something else about it."

Now all the curiosity turned toward Alice.

"Linda said she's pretty sure he didn't leave alone," she said. "Apparently Sunny Day thought she could get ahead better with John than by working at the inn."

"Oh, dear," Gwen remarked. "Are you all right with that?"

Alice shrugged. "Mostly I'm glad it's not me—although I feel a little sorry for her."

"I suspect," Gwen said, "that she's a girl who knows how to land on her feet. I wouldn't worry too much."

Annie watched her best friend closely as Alice shrugged. When she was convinced Alice really was fine, she smiled. This had been a strange mystery, and she was glad to have it settled.

Stella spoke up. "You know, if we hurry, we still might make it to the dance performance. Instead of being part of a plan, it can be a kind of celebration."

When everyone agreed, Annie glanced down at her clothes. "I'm dressed a little casually," she said, smoothing a hand over the A-line corduroy skirt.

"It's not formal," Alice insisted, tugging on her friend's arm.

"And you look very nice," Ian threw in.

So she let them hustle her out the front door. As she turned for one last glance at Grey Gables, she smiled as she pictured Gram standing on the porch, happy to see her beloved granddaughter surrounded by such good friends.